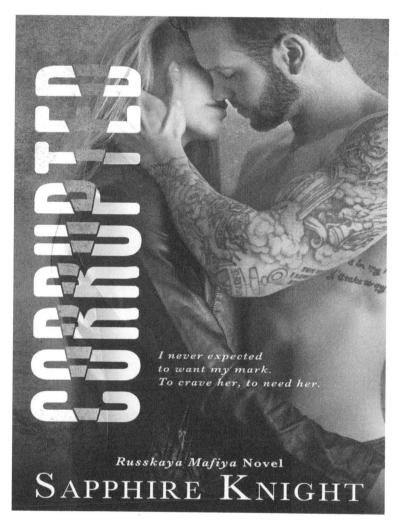

CORRUPTED

*I never expected
to want my mark.
To crave her, to need her.*

Russkaya Mafiya Novel

SAPPHIRE KNIGHT

Table of Contents

Corrupted

Copyright © 2015 by Sapphire Knight

Warning:

This novel includes graphic language and adult situations. It may be offensive to some readers and includes situations that may be hotspots for certain individuals. This book is intended for ages 17 and older due to steamy, sexy, hotness that will have you jumping your man. This work is fictional. The story is meant to entertain the reader and may not always be completely accurate. Any reproduction of these works without Author Sapphire Knight's written consent is pirating and will be punished to the fullest extent of the law. Stealing this book makes you a thieving prick and I hope your tits fall off.

This book is fiction.

The guys are over the top Alphas.

My men and women are nuts.

This is not real.

Don't steal my shit, I have bills too.

Read for enjoyment.

This is not your momma's cookbook.

Easily offended people should not read this.

Acknowledgements-

My husband- I love you.

My boys- You are my whole world. I love you both.

The lovely Beta readers, Thank you- Tamra for picking up on the things I completely breeze over and writing reviews I can't wait to read. You each stepped up to the plate and have given me valuable feedback. I love it that you can be straight with me and then be great friends also!

My Editor

Sapphire's Naughty Princesses- Thank you ladies for everything you do to help promote my work, for all of your support and encouragement. You make me want to write even more!

My blogger friends-There are so many to list and for that I am in awe.

My readers- Thank you for making this possible for me. I wish I could hug each one of you!

Prologue

Warm, syrupy liquid coats my fingers, bleeding onto my hands and drips to the cold cement below. The sky is black, the stars and moon hiding, helping me complete my task. The calming *swoosh* of the waves mask my noises as I drop the lifeless body to the ground to finish securing weights to his limbs.

The small pier is deserted and the men on the docks know to mind their own business. No one wants to be involved with the Bratva, especially when its leader is dumping bodies. They keep their concerns to themselves, knowing they would be next on my list.

I relish the power.

I was the smart one, the one strictly handling the money of the business. Then my uncle gave me my first taste of disposal. I don't necessarily enjoy the kill itself, but I love watching them sink into the deep, murky waters of the lakes surrounding us.

Chapter 1

Elaina

"Just a minute!" I grumble at the drunk asshole waiting for me at the end of the bar. Geez, my feet are killing me. I sling another vodka-seven and set it in front of Tate's big brother, Viktor. Rushing to the other end of the bar, I address said drunk.

"Yes, sir?"

"Yeah! Umm, gimme ah beer! Yeah, beer!" he chortles, lazily lying the top half of his body across the bar. Ugh, men like this make me sick.

"Sorry but you've had a bit much to drink and I can't serve you any more alcohol." I try to keep it polite, when in reality I want to get the soda gun and spray this idiot with the nappy hair.

"I'm the paying customer here! This is bullshit. Give me a beer!"

"Look, you can have a glass of water or I can make up a pot of coffee, but no more beer. I'm sorry," I yell over the pulsing music. His rancid breath washes over me and I gag slightly.

"You're sorry, huh? Good for nothin' fucking cunt." He spits the words out angrily and it takes every bone in my body to stay professional. Being a bartender I know I will deal with assholes but I'm no one's door mat.

"When you calm down, then I will get you some water."

He reaches over the bar, grabbing onto my mid-length, blonde hair, "Calm? Get over here, I'll show you calm!" My head snaps back, and with the pain I'm immediately thrown into another time of my life.

***

Elaina, ten years old...

"Where are you going, baby girl? Daddy wants to talk to you for a second."

"I'm sorry, but I have to go to bed. I have to get up early for school," I reply, trying to make a decent excuse to escape his clutches.

"I only need you for a few minutes there, baby girl. Come here."

I squirm uncomfortably. "Umm, please, I'm really tired." Brent likes to get close and touch me. It makes me feel weird and I don't like it.

"I said NOW, Elaina." His voice is menacing as he reaches his large fingers towards his belt and dutifully releases the clasp. Brent wraps his hand around the thick leather, pulling it free from the charcoal grey suit pants. Looking at me longingly, he reaches out and grasps my blonde hair roughly. The action forces my head back and my eyes crest with tears. *Ouch, please, no.*

At a creak in the floor, he glances up quickly, taken by surprise.

"Brent, what's going on? Was she bad again?"

My eyes rapidly scan the room until they fall on my foster mom, Paige. Thank God, she came at just the right time. She's standing in the doorway with her hand on her hip, glaring at me spitefully. She always looks at me like that.

He speaks through gritted teeth, "She was talking back again." He sits up to adjust himself.

Brent releases my hair at the same time as he propels me forward, dropping the belt to the floor. I stumble, splaying my arms out wildly to catch myself. I tend to be a little bit of a klutz sometimes and I've gotten pretty used to grabbing for anything within reach when I start to go down.

Paige grabs my shoulder and I cringe at the pain. Tightening my tummy, I hold my breath.

"Come along, Elaina. Such a pretty little girl. It's a shame you are so ugly inside and can't behave properly. We certainly won't be keeping you."

Paige walks me quickly down the long hall to a small room I'm staying in. I shuffle my feet hastily along the plain, tan carpet to keep up with her pace. "Now, go to bed and don't make a sound," she tells me sternly and shoves my small frame inside the shoebox-sized bedroom.

The door swings closed and I jump out of the way before it hits me. There's a loud *click* as she locks the door. She doesn't realize it, but I enjoy that sound. As long as that door is locked, I know I won't have to submit myself to being uncomfortable around them. I know as long as Paige has the key, the lock will keep *him* out.

I shed my jean shorts for my pajama bottoms. I swear it always feels like someone is watching me; I wonder if there are ghosts in this house or something? Sighing loudly, I lie in the single-sized bed provided to me with the bright yellow comforter. The blanket is the only happy thing about this room. Is this what it's like for normal kids? Do their parents treat them like these people treat me?

***

As I snap out of it, wheezing with shock, I see Viktor crushing the drunk onto the bar top, whispering something in the man's ear. The drunk man shakes his head rapidly, sending his shaggy hair in every direction.

"No, no please. I swear it, I swear never again. I won't even look her way, man, I swear it!" he sputters, sounding surprisingly sober and Viktor says something in Russian, nodding at the man beside him in black. Viktor straightens up, adjusting the jacket of his suit and steps out of the way.

The guy next to Viktor bends swiftly and grasps the drunk harshly, forcing him from the bar stool and carts him off towards the back of the club. The drunk drags his feet, begging the guard to reconsider.

Viktor brushes off his suit jacket, annoyed, and shrugs so the sleeves drop back in place. As he comes around the bar, he has completely returned to his ever professional façade. He's always so well put together, so handsome and stern. The word *dashing* suits him perfectly as if he could step straight into a movie and fit right in. He'd easily take on the lead role.

He steps carefully across the slippery floor behind the bar, not scuffing the expensive shoes decorating his feet, until he is a mere twelve inches away from me. He gazes at me, with an expression full of concern.

Viktor's eyes can be filled with menace at times, though he's shown me nothing but kindness since I first woke up out of my hospital haze over a year ago. Another horrible memory to add to my list; unfortunately that one was my own doing.

"Are you...?" he starts to ask. Puzzled, I tilt my head. He brushes his hand tenderly down the side of my arm and peers into my eyes, trying to gauge how I am.

I clear my throat loudly. "Uh, yeah, I'm okay." It comes out a tad gruff for me but I'm still a bit overwhelmed.

He nods minutely and bites the side of his lip. He regards each crevice of my face, watching, reading my features for any clues. He won't find anything, I've been hiding my feelings about many things, those for him included, for far too long. I do care about him as a friend and of course he *is* devastatingly good looking with his strong Russian features.

I blink rapidly a few times and step back, "Sorry, that guy just caught me off-guard."

He can't be touching me like that. I don't know what to think when he touches me so I shuffle backwards more and try to collect my bearings. I turn away from him, effectively putting up my protective wall.

He simply nods, clenches his fist and makes his way back to his seat at the end of the bar.

I quickly walk to the opposite side of the bar to tend to the other customers. 007 is a very busy club, but thankfully only special orders come to the bartender. With the unlimited drinks here, included in the huge door fee, there is always a drunken guy being a dick at some point.

After growing up in foster homes it really doesn't bother me. I have met my fair share of assholes trying to take advantage of me. I guess I feel like there is this barrier, like they can't get to me because of the large bar between us. It's probably naïve of me to feel that way but I do.

At least here there's some sort of monitoring; Viktor always takes care of any issues I may have. He doesn't know just how grateful I am for that. I try to keep those things to myself though.

I don't want to appear weak to any man. I've definitely gone through my fair share and I have learned a man will take full advantage of any sign of weakness. Viktor doesn't know just how scared I get when someone crosses that line.

I glimpse over at him nonchalantly while refilling the four napkin stations placed randomly on top of the bar. He's beautiful. My sister is so lucky to have married someone who looks like Viktor. He is tall, and strong; not the beefed up strong, but solid enough to easily carry me out of the bar over his shoulder. I know that much for sure since he's done it a few times.

Vik is dressed in a crisp suit each time I see him. His clothes fit as if they were made specifically for him. With his money though, I wouldn't be surprised if they were custom made. We could be running an errand and yet he still dresses so formally, I tend to look like a bum next to him.

Personally, as long as I'm wearing clean clothes and they are comfortable, I'm good. He says appearances are important. However, when you are deep in mafia territory I doubt it really matters. He could be wearing a tank top and board shorts, but if they see Viktor, they know he is the king ding-a-ling around here besides Tate.

His hair is short, complimented by a proud nose, almost as if he were bred to be stuck up. He's not though. Viktor's just observant and quiet.

His eyes are the same as Tate's. They're a gorgeous hazel, except a little more on the green side. Viktor's also older at twenty-seven, and acts every bit of it. I rarely see him smile unless I pop off and say something amusing.

I swallow as I take in his five o'clock shadow. He shouldn't be allowed to look so good; it's not fair to other men.

I'm caught blatantly staring as he looks over at me and our irises meet—his hazel to my sparkly blues. I blush and turn away. No more gawking, it's time to finish up my shift.

Viktor

I sit observing her, every single shift. Each time she's here, she wears a tight little skirt that hugs her hips. It's glued to her like a second skin. I feel as if the skirt has a leash on me, taunting me every time she passes me to serve someone else. Then there are the times she bends over cleaning or digging out more supplies and I'm met with the smooth skin on the backs of her thighs. I would insist she wear pants but I fear they would outline her ass perfectly and be just as taxing on my libido.

Her sweet little smiles I get on occasion are payment enough for sitting here, putting up with obnoxious drunks. I don't mind a few drinks. However, when you are in here all the time and act abhorrent, I have no patience.

Every week I corner the manager for her schedule, so I can be here with her. I threaten him each time with being fired. I know he secretly looks at her, wants her, and fantasizes about her. He's lucky I do not kill him for it. If she were mine, I would hurt him.

She may be stubborn and believe I am bothersome, but I have to be. Ever since that day I was sent to dispose of her, it was like something in me demanded to protect her. I've never looked at a woman before and felt as if I was literally pulled toward her.

I cherish that day in the hospital, her lying there helpless and sweet. The taste of her skin, her scent, even tainted with the after smell of alcohol made me want her desperately. I promised Emily I wouldn't let anyone harm her sister and I meant it. Now that she is Tate's wife, she is also like a little sister to me.

In the past I have hinted to Elaina about my feelings, but she hasn't taken me seriously. I feel as if I'm a desperate fool, constantly lusting after her. Not once has Elaina made a move to show she wants to be more than just friends. It's crushing, but I still hold out for her with each shift she works.

She zigzags behind the bar, working in haste. I love how her cheeks flush with a fine mist of perspiration. I can picture her beautifully, riding me, covered in that same pink blush. Perhaps her ass is pink too, with a few of my handprints. She looks like the type of sweet girl who could use a few spankings.

She is a hard worker and I admire how well she handles customers. 007 is lucky to have her as an employee. The men here should be paying me just to watch her work the bar.

I offered once to take care of her. She brushed it off as if the idea were ludicrous. Taking in her loveliness, it's far from ridiculous.

In Russia when I was a small boy, we were taught to look for splendor, so it's natural for me to gravitate towards her. She is all beauty. She encompasses the all-American, girl-next-door look.

She's perfect with her freckles and blue eyes. With her corn-colored blonde hair she screams American, but if it were a few shades lighter, she could definitely pass as a Russian girl.

At least I know that if Mother were to ever meet her there would not be any issues, since she adores Emily. God, that dinner prior to Tate and Emily's wreck was hilarious. I thought our mother was going to pull her hair out and then spit on Emily. I couldn't stop chuckling at the little comments she kept making. I knew Tate was a goner as soon as I saw them get out of the car. He had an almost feral look when I greeted Emily. Frankly, I'm surprised he let Mother get away with as much as she did.

Mishka is the one I would really want Elaina to meet if I had a choice. She was always more of a mother to Tate and me growing up. She cooked for us, got us ready for our private school and even slapped us on occasion if we were out of control. Mother didn't dare touch us or my father would have gone ballistic, but Mishka would have busted Papa's knees. Tate had to get his knee fetish from somewhere.

I know my father would call Elaina a princess, as she resembles such. However, that trash will never meet her, I'll make sure of it. He may be my father, but he died to me when he double crossed me and my brother. He is fortunate we let him live this long.

Have you ever met someone and just known there was something about them? That's exactly how I felt the first time I heard her speak to me from that hospital bed.

I was already drawn to her, to her beauty and sweet smell. Then her soft, sweet voice sounded like a melody and it was like my eyes were opened for the first time to this love at first sight notion. Now each time she talks to me, I hear that harmony and it brings a little bit of bliss into my stressful life.

None of it matters though, as she couldn't care less if I sat here. She has told me many times she is a grown up and can take care of herself. She may be independent, but deep inside she needs me, I know it.

When she wrecked her car into my brother's she was extremely drunk. She tried to get crazy the last time London, Avery and Emily all came to 007. Luckily, I'd brought her and was able to take her home safely. She is careless and it drives me mad. How can such a perfect creature not take better care of herself?

I turn away from her as Alexei, my guard, approaches me. I'm still sipping on my vodka-seven Elaina prepared for me. She's passable at making drinks, not great, but okay. I won't be drinking her martinis anytime soon, though.

"Boss," he says quietly, scanning our surroundings.

"What is it, Alexei?"

"I dumped him out back. Are you sure?" he double checks. He really is a diligent employee and I enjoy him working for me, but I have to keep them all on their toes.

"You question me?" I stare him down crazily. "He touched her. Yes. Take care of it, or I will," I snap, annoyed.

"Very good, sir. Consider it done," he replies and stands to his full height. He isn't a big man, maybe six foot or so like I am. He may have me beat muscle wise, but I've been training for most of my life in killing methods.

I gesture with my hand, indifferent. "Take him to the docks. Feed him to the rats."

"Yes, Boss," he replies, unfazed, and strides toward the back entrance.

The punishment may appear harsh, but everyone in here who watched what happened with her needs to see. They will witness Alexei leave through the back and know that the drunk will never return.

They will learn she belongs to the Solntsvskaya Bratva. To the boss, to me. Even if she's unaware of it, they won't be.

Hawk, the manager of Taint is here filling in. He's a decent employee, but I prefer it when Elaina works with another female. I take special notice each time Elaina talks to Hawk, trying to work out what exactly they are saying. Unfortunately for me though, I can't read lips very well.

I can't stand it when he leans in close, or touches her. I want to fire him each time he lays his hand on her sun-kissed arm. I hold myself back though. I know she wouldn't forgive me for acting so petty.

I tend to take stock when she speaks to any male who isn't just there for a quick bar transaction. Hawk's here to fill in for one of the other bartenders who was meant to relieve Elaina, but called in sick. Of course I already know this from the manager informing me earlier, but act oblivious to it.

She gives him a small side-hug and a smile, then grabs her purse. She's getting ready to leave, throwing the sling of her purse carelessly over her shoulder as she comes to me. Sitting up straight, I wipe my features clean of any dark thoughts and concentrate on her lightness.

She flashes me a small smile and a little wave as she shouts over the noise, "Goodbye, Viktor. Thank you for earlier."

I can't help but stare into her eyes. I may seem like a stalker but it's like getting lost in a sea of blue and I can't help myself.

"Have a good evening, Elaina." I keep it formal, not acknowledging her thanks. She should just forget what happened. I run the Bratva. That was peas compared to what I normally deal with. She doesn't seem to realize I would do so much more for her if she were to ask.

She gives me a shaky smile and heads toward the door to the club. I gesture to Spartak who's been watching me closely, waiting for the signal. I nod toward her and he quickly follows.

Spartak will trail her home to her crappy little apartment and make sure she is safe. It'll be his job to park outside her building and keep watch. Spar's her unofficial guard. I know it's not a practical thing to have my men do, but it's a new requirement of them and no one ever said I was reasonable.

I leave to go home too because if she's not at the club then I don't want to be there either. I live close to Tate, in the same gated community. My house is tan with decorative landscaping.

When I bought my home, Mishka came over right away with a list of plants she wanted. The guards went and picked up everything she asked for. That crazy, old woman came and worked in the yard for a week straight. It looks beautiful, but I'm just thankful I only have to worry about the sprinkler being on and nothing else.

Tate's backyard is absurd. Mishka and Emily are always changing it up and planting new flowers everywhere. I wouldn't be surprised if my little brother fattens up with all the cooking Mishka is teaching Emily.

On the plus side, I can visit now and eat a good dinner. My brother and I can cook fairly well, but we always just grill at night. Mishka will make delicious old Russian recipes.

Thankfully, the trip is short. My house is only about ten minutes from the club. I love my sporty James Bond type cars parked in the garage, but I'm too exhausted to really enjoy them today.

Running a bunch of criminals makes you age inside quickly and my uncle has always told me to drive a car you love. He says we have too many things to worry about, that we need to have something we can enjoy in the small amount of free time we have.

I pull my black Mercedes-AMG GT S into my three car garage, next to my Jaguar. My Mercedes purrs like a pleased kitten, enjoying the attention, but god do I love my Jaguar. My Jag doesn't purr, no, she growls when I give her gas. Maybe I'll take her for a drive after I rest for a while.

I'm greeted by a silent house and it's refreshing. Leaning my head back, I close my eyes tightly for a moment and breathe in the clean air. *Ahh.* That's nice after the noisy club for the past five hours.

As I strut leisurely to my office I shuck my jacket and shoes, diligently unbuttoning my shirt. One thing I thoroughly enjoy about being home is the lack of clothes.

I sit in my comfortable, overly plush leather desk chair and fill a tumbler with Grey Goose. Growing up around my uncle, I learned to drink vodka as if it was water. Now it's second nature to have it at home when I'm relaxing.

Taking a deep breath, I'm met with the vibration of my personal cell phone ringing. This better be important. If it were the ringtone to the business phone I would let it keep ringing. I glance at the flashing screen to see it's Tate.

"Braat," I answer 'brother' in Russian on the second ring.

The majority of our conversations are in Russian, even though Tate hates when I call any attention to our native language. I am proud to be Russian and use it to my advantage when I talk business.

"Viktor. What went on at the club today?"

"I'm well, brother, thank you for inquiring."

"Save it, Viktor, what happened?" he asks, frustration coating his voice.

"Nothing happened."

"Bullshit! I heard you took a man out the back door, is this true?"

"Yes, and? What is it to you, Luka? I had business, it was handled."

"Business! Are you joking? You carried a man out the back door in front of customers! That is reckless, Viktor. You are being too bold."

"Bold, Luka? No. You forget that I was the one handed the Mafiya, but gave it to you. You may be the Big Boss now, but I run the rest. The only thing *bold*, is you speaking out of place. Mind your business, Luka. I will handle things as I please."

"Viktor, you will go to jail if the wrong person sees this. I know you stepped down, but at the same time I stepped up into a position you so desperately ran from. Don't you lecture me about giving up your spot. I took it for you so you could have freedom, yet you embrace the Bratva for Uncle."

"Yes, someone has to embrace the dirty deeds of our family. I clean up messes, Luka, it's what I do. The trash put his hands on Elaina at the bar and I was fixing the issue, little brother."

"Why didn't you tell me that in the first place, instead of fighting with me? We have to stick together, Vik. With father out, it's you and me, now."

"I know this, it will be fine, Luka. Don't stress, I am doing my part."

"Thank you, and if you need anything, call."

"I will, if it comes to that."

I hang up and pound my fist on my desk, shaking the glass of vodka. My little brother has some nerve, getting angry with me. He has no idea what he's talking about. I wonder which little rat called him.

Truth? I didn't take over the Mafiya because I knew my father really wanted Tate to have it. He always favored Tate over myself and that was fine, I had my uncle. I stepped down to make my father happy. Had I known what he was doing to Tate and me, then I would have taken it over and not had the burden placed on my little brother. Should have known he wouldn't think twice to lie to his sons. He's a slimy two-faced fish and doesn't deserve the air he breathes.

Tate went ballistic when he found out about our father being even more crooked than he had suspected. He knows I had worked very hard to make all the books appear legit. They weren't legit but I altered them in good faith that I was helping my father change his ways.

Tate doesn't mind being in guns, but he loathes the drug and sex trade. I don't mind the drugs and my men make plenty of money from them. I do not dabble in the sex trade; however, that stopped when I took charge. I know my uncle was incredibly supportive of it, but I can't fathom selling another human being.

Drugs are another thing entirely. I feel the person has the choice. If they choose to be a user, that's on them. The same with gambling; we have many circuits of gambling that we support and profit from, also the occasional gambling debt one might incur. I have no problem lending and having my men collect my interest due.

I still handle some disposal. I know I don't have to, that I have men for it, but I enjoy it. I guess it's just another mess for me to clean up.

I take a large drink of my vodka and call my guard, to check on Elaina.

"Spartak?"

"She's good, Boss, just stopped by a little store on the way and got a few things."

"Alcohol?"

"No, sir, just snacks."

"Very good. Pay attention."

"Yes, of course, sir," he replies diligently and I hang up. I pull up her number to send her the nightly text I've sent since I first took her home.

Me: Good Night, Princess

I'm met with the only response I have ever gotten from her at night. One evening I hope she will add an endearment to it, but I won't hold my breath.

Princess: Night.

Chapter 2

Elaina
Two days later...

I wake with a start. *Fuck.* Another bad dream.

The dreams have never stopped. I had to live through everything with Brent and now I'm stuck dreaming about it. I don't want to remember.

God, that dream was so vivid. It felt like he really was touching me again and my skin crawls with the aftereffects. Gagging, I take a few deep breaths to try and calm my nerves.

It always felt wrong each time. I didn't really know it was immoral until I got older and saw how my friends' parents interacted with them. Their parents treated them completely differently than what I was used to. I think back to when I started to question things.

***

I was thirteen and staying the night at my girlfriend's house. I had never been allowed to stay away but Brent and Paige went out of town. I got to stay with Stephanie for three days.

Stephanie's house was a two story, warmly decorated home and her family was the kindest I had ever met. Each night I lay beside her in her big bed with its fluffy pink comforter. I was always waiting, scared for her father to come in, but he never did.

Finally, I worked up the nerve and asked Stephanie if he came to lie beside her when I wasn't there. I thought perhaps it was my fault, disturbing what fathers do with their daughters.

I remember she had looked at me like I had lost my mind. Stephanie then drilled it into my head that fathers don't normally lie with their daughters, especially when they are older.

She never told anyone about that, but we did start to grow apart. I didn't understand at the time why she drifted away, but I did once I got older. I didn't blame Stephanie, I was dirty and no one wanted to be around that. I never spoke of it to anyone again. I couldn't stand the thought of my case worker finding out.

Brent and Paige were small worries compared to what some foster parents put kids through. I could handle Paige being mean and saying hateful things. I could even deal with Brent and his touching, I had to.

As soon as I was old enough to leave without the cops picking me up, I split. I had been working a part time job after school and on the weekends at the Dollar Store close by. I was saving every penny and delighted in the time spent away from that house. I got my crappy apartment after some time and eventually was able to get my car. It was rough, but I refused to sink.

***

Shaking off those ominous feelings, I head into the shower. I scrub extra hard, attempting to remove the feeling I have crawling all over my skin. Turning the faucet to hot, the water heats quickly and I get a tingle from the burning. The pain helps clear my mind of some of the details. My skin turns bright pink, but it's better than the creepy crawlies I had before. I'll take the pain over memories of that sick fuck any day.

Raiding my small closet, I throw on my short jean skirt, one of the few nice tank tops Emily gave me and the boots I borrowed from her. Not my usual style but the guys at the bar seem to eat it up. Any extra tips I can make by wearing a skirt or borrowing boots, I'm going to take full advantage of.

Thank God I have Emily now. I had no idea how much a sister could truly impact my life and make things better. I'm even more excited about the fact of becoming an aunty.

My car is almost paid off, thankfully. It seems like all I do is work and pay my bills. I'll occasionally go on a drinking binge or party but that's about all. I can't afford much more even if I wanted to. It's okay, this life is way better than the one I had growing up. I just have to keep my ducks in a row and keep my eyes on the prize—being car payment free.

I'm usually too afraid of getting close to any guys and them touching me, unless I drink. If I'm toasted, I'll let them kiss me or grab my breast, but that's as far as I've ever let it go. I get creeped out and reminded of how it felt when Brent would mess with me.

People don't understand that sexual assault of any kind can affect the victim for the rest of their lives. I may not have been raped or anything that serious but this still impacts my daily life, no matter how strong I feel I've become. I've read online that it's a form of PTSD. I don't think I really have it, but I do have my triggers. Not like I'm going to visit a doctor anytime soon and discuss it with them.

I'm fortunate working at the club and having Viktor there. He has no idea just how much I appreciate him looking out for me all the time. Not only do I feel safer but I'm able to work at a high end club. It helps dramatically with me meeting my goal of paying off my debts. I never want to be that vulnerable again, of being in a position I can't escape if I need to.

Tate is drastically protective of my sister, Emily, and with Viktor doing little things for me, I figure it's probably a family trait. I know very little about his family besides the stuff Emily has told me. She's not very forthcoming about them though. I know they both have a group of scary-looking guards. For what reason, who knows? My guess is because they are rich and because of all the Mafia-ish people in this area.

I grab a banana on my way to my white Camaro. It's all I can afford right now, so I make do. It's not the fancy version of the Camaro and it's not even that new, but I love her. She's good to me and I do my best to take care of her. I'm thankful I can park my car close to my apartment and right under a light every night as I get a little spooked in the dark around here.

I take a large bite, stuffing my mouth with a third of the banana. I'm hungrier than I first thought. I wipe the banana off my fingers onto the towel next to me after I climb into the car. I start her up, loving the little rumble she makes; it's almost as if she thinks she's fast.

Glancing in my rearview mirror, I drop my banana and shriek in surprise. *What the fuck?* One of Viktor's thugs is standing directly behind my car. I shut the engine off and climb out quickly. *What a waste of a good banana, damn it!*

I snap rudely, "Umm, can I help you?"

This is it, Viktor has overstepped the boundary this time. We formed a small friendship when I was in the hospital. I've tried pulling away but he just keeps pushing me. This time he's out of line and I plan to give him a thorough piece of my mind. I place my hands on my hips and cock them to the side, tapping my foot. This better be good.

"Forgive me, ma'am," he says with a slight Russian accent. "I am Spartak." He smiles warmly and my anger melts slightly.

"Okay, Spartak, what's going on? You're in my way."

"Ma'am, please, your tire is bad, may I fix?" he asks, gesturing to my back tire on the passenger side. I walk around the rear end and look at him skeptically at the same time. I glance at the tire.

"Shit! What am I supposed to do with this?" I flail my arms toward the very flat tire and cringe.

I have to get to work soon or I will be late. There's no way I have time to get a new tire and I definitely shouldn't drive it like this. I'll have to call a cab and that's going to be so expensive.

"I fix it for you." His Russian gets a little stronger and I'm immediately reminded of my sister's good friend, Nikoli.

"You can fix it? How?"

He walks to the trunk and gestures for me to open it. I press the trunk release button on my key fob and he proceeds to show me where the spare is. He also shows me how to remove it from the trunk, what the jack is, and how to jack my car up. Then he takes the old tire off, puts my spare on and loads the flat back into the trunk for me.

I'm in awe that this man just offered to help me and do all of this work. It took him about twenty minutes total. He did it efficiently and never once made me feel guilty for his help.

I never could have changed it that fast, once I figured out what to do. I cataloged each maneuver so I have it for future reference. I like being able to do stuff and not having to depend on someone else all the time.

I clap my hands happily and smile. "Wow, thank you so much! Do you want some money, for umm, fixing this?"

"No, no, ma'am. Please just go to work, I don't want you to be late." He gestures with his hands for me to get in the car. I nod and climb inside.

The flat tire sucks, I'll have to pay for that eventually. At least I'm not out a cab fare and since I leave early, I should be right on time.

That was so nice! What a friendly guy; I wish there were more people out there willing to jump in and help someone else. I have to tell Viktor his guy was so polite and helpful. Wait, why was his man here anyhow?

There's no telling with Viktor, and I plan to ask as soon as I see him.

After a short non-eventful drive, I arrive and it's my favorite time in the club. There isn't anyone here besides the manager and Viktor's guy who changed my tire. He ended up following me here and opened the door for me. It's kind of neat feeling like I have my own personal assistant, but creepy at the same time.

I check the place over, then turn on lights and fans for the main room, storage and the bathrooms. I enjoy opening the club up, makes me feel really useful.

I wonder where Viktor is today. He's normally here eating his dinner or lunch from some random restaurant. It's amazing he's in such great shape with always eating out. I wonder... could Vik not know how to cook? I really want to ask his guy here about him, but at the same time I don't want to seem too eager.

An hour passes with me busily chopping up lemons, limes, oranges and refilling the maraschino cherries. I usually have opening shift and do the prep. I get paid fifteen dollars an hour for doing prep, which is amazing. Every place I've worked at required you to do it, while paying you a measly two dollars an hour. The only thing I hate about opening is filling the ice bin. Lugging the ice bucket back and forth gets heavy after a few trips. The later shifts all have a bar back that does that kind of stuff.

The other bartenders and floor guys start arriving and the music gets cranked loud while everyone sets up their own stations.

I've been doing everything I can in the past hour to stay busy, but it's driving me crazy! Viktor is never late and he never misses a shift that I work. It's like he's a part of the whole shift. We barely speak to each other but we exchange glances about a million times a night. I have to at least make sure he's okay. Yep, that's my excuse, and I'm going to use it.

I throw my towel down on the beer cooler and quickly round the large bar. I go searching through the club to find Viktor's guy. Spartak, I think he said his name was.

Busily looking everywhere but in front of me, I run straight into something solid.

"Oof," I yelp.

Large hands grab my arms to steady me and I look up, glancing over a leather vest that says in bold letters *Enforcer* on one side and *Ares* on the other side. It's followed by massive shoulders, a thick neck and finally a stern but friendly face.

"Uh?"

"Careful, doll, you ran straight into me. Say, do you know where I can find the owner?" he asks in a gruff voice. I stare like a deer trapped in the headlights. He looks at me curiously, slowly peeling his hands off my arms and steps back, cocking his eyebrow, "Doll?"

"Yes! No, I mean sorry. I don't see him much."

He nods and smiles slightly. Wow, scary to gorgeous with just a small smile. How do men do that so easily?

"Alright, bet." He walks past me and I have to stop to catch my breath for a second.

I watch him walk down the hall; his beefy back has a large symbol reading 'Oath Keepers MC'. I've got to remember to tell Tate if I see him, and what on earth does 'bet' mean?

I continue on my journey until I spot Spartak propped up against the wall near the office, "Ma'am?" he queries when he sees me approach.

"Hi, Spartak. I was just wondering, can I ask you a question?"

"Yes."

"Okay, umm. Where's Viktor?"

"Why, is there something you need? I can help or fix it."

"No, it's not that. He's just normally here. I was wondering if he was coming."

He smirks a little when I ask if Viktor's coming. No doubt he's going to tell him about it. "He couldn't be here, so I'm here to watch over you."

"To watch over me? You have got to be joking!"

"No, ma'am, I'm not. I'm here in case you need anything."

"Well, Viktor always sits at the bar," I reply tartly and spin on my boot heels. I storm back to the bar in a huff.

That man has some serious nerve, planting someone to monitor me. So Viktor really is here each shift to watch me! I knew it. I have no idea how to deal with this whole stalking situation.

I grab the towel back up and wipe the bar top thoroughly trying to scrub some of my frustration out. A few minutes pass and I hear a stool scrape. I look over to see Spartak posted at the end of the bar where Viktor usually sits. I hate to admit, but seeing him sitting there does bring me some comfort. It's not as much as Viktor, but it'll do.

Viktor

Tapping my fingers on my desk to a beat in my head, I sit bored at one of my warehouses down by Tellico Lake. We have a front set up as if we store boat and lake supplies. However the crates in here are not filled with anything remotely close to skis or life preservers. Actually, quite the opposite; I house guns, knives, drugs, any of that sort in my storage buildings. I have them spread all over this area of Tennessee. I simply look like a productive businessman with a lot of merchandise for the different lakes.

My uncle came up with the idea years ago. We've had great success with it. Not to mention, Tate and I combined own many cops in the state as a back-up plan. We still get the occasional new curious face popping in though.

The door leading to my office slams. It has to be Alexei coming to report to me. I have a main reinforced metal door you have to get through before you can get to my real office door. You can never be too careful when dealing with criminals.

Alexei's one of the few with the access code to get back here. I've known him for many years and he helps me a lot. I trust him more than I should, but I never let anyone else know that.

"Boss?" he calls out and knocks on the door, staying in the hall.

He's trained well. I have very little tolerance for foolishness. I'm in charge of this organization, I expect respect. This isn't some after schoolboys club I run around here.

"Yes, Alexei, come in."

My brother worries that I keep things so formal, and that I have no friends. He doesn't realize I deal with a different crowd in my businesses. Keeping things formal keeps my eyes open and my heart beating.

Alexei enters and I gesture to the chair seated in front of my desk. He adjusts his suit and sits. Being around me frequently, he is required to dress the part and is usually in a suit or occasionally black military style cargo pants and black fitted tank top. It all depends on what job he's performing.

He's a very valuable asset to me but every chance I get I have to make it known he can be replaced. My uncle taught me it will make people work harder trying to please you and so far that has held true. Of course I do reward them with a few perks when acknowledgment is due.

"Boss, the specialty weapons you were waiting on from Russia arrived."

"Very good, any issues arise with it?"

"No, sir, it went smoothly."

"Good, I love when a plan is executed correctly and it comes together as intended. Those weapons will bring in a large profit. Make sure you call the Columbians that were interested in them and let them know it's now an option. Tell me, how did it go with the man from the bar?"

"The drunk was no problem either. I shot him up with heroin and fed him to the rats as you asked. He screamed for a while and I made sure the big body pieces left over were dumped. I'll call the Columbians today and get the weapons taken care of."

I nod my approval. I'm pretty impressed he hasn't called me for instructions or anything. He's just taken initiative and completed everything that needed doing. It's such a relief to be able to at least rely on one person around here now that my uncle is out of the business.

"Very good. I am pleased, Alexei. What's next?"

"Thank you, Boss. I do have a guy here waiting to talk to you."

"Who's here?"

"The gambling guy I told you about a few days ago. He's just like the rest, acting like he doesn't need the money when he wants it really bad."

"All right, search him then escort him back," I say and he jumps up quickly to get the customer.

After a few seconds he arrives with an older, average-sized man. The guy's sporting neatly trimmed brown hair, a big nose, khaki pleated pants, and a pale blue Ralph Lauren polo shirt. He looks the part of your typical businessman douche.

He stands in front of my desk appearing rather intimidated. "Mr. Masterson, thank you for meeting with me," he states graciously and I gesture to the chair. Alexei stands between the door and the man.

"No problem, Mr...?

"Yes, sir, I'm Brent Tollfree, nice to meet you," he utters nervously in a strong southern accent.

Brent reminds me of some of the older southern films my mother liked to watch when we first moved to the States. She believed it would help her understand people better when they spoke, I just thought it was a waste of time.

"Okay, what exactly can I do for you?"

"Well, I would like to take out a personal loan."

Refraining from rolling my eyes and scoffing, I nod. "All right, how much were you looking to borrow and what do you have as collateral?" I probe and he fidgets a little in his chair.

I love watching grown men squirm when they realize they are about to make a deal with the Bratva. They might as well be signing a contract with the Devil. We don't pride ourselves in being good and kind but in being strong and ruthless.

"Can I borrow sixty thousand?" he queries quietly, cocking his head and Alexei whistles at the amount. Alexei's quite the businessman and knows how to play the game well.

"Well, let me see, you got referred to me by your colleague who has had a loan with me, correct?" I inquire and he nods. "What can you provide as collateral?"

"I have a Cadillac Escalade I can give you if it comes to that."

"Oh, Mr. Tollfree, I will be taking a lot more than your car if it gets to that point." I steeple my fingers and wait for him to decide his fate.

It only takes a few seconds, but then that's normal for everyone coming to borrow money.

"I understand, Mr. Masterson. It won't come to that. Thank you, thanks so much," he declares graciously and I give in, rolling my eyes. I deal with these types of people all the time and they are all the same. I wave my hand toward him and Alexei signals to the guy to get up.

"Alexei can get you that money, since it's not much."

"Okay, thank you so much, Mr. Masterson, I really appreciate it." I nod, already aggravated and Alexei rushes him out of my office. He's lucky he quit talking or I may have just cut his tongue out. *Annoying little piss ant.*

I'll probably have to make my men pay him a visit in about three months when he conveniently forgets to repay that loan he wanted so badly. I remember his buddy well. I thought I was going to have a new body to dump when his father came to his rescue.

Gamblers are the worst, always looking for that quick buck. It usually ends up costing them everything.

I wonder how the beautiful princess is doing today. I loathe the fact I'm missing her shift. This is the first that I've missed and it's all I can think about. I have to take care of my businesses though. I hope one day she allows me to make her my priority above everything else.

Alexei comes rushing back into my office interrupting my pleasant thoughts of Elaina. My stomach drops at the sight of him. I'm stunned, gaping; he never enters unannounced and yelling loudly.

"Boss! Boss!" He is bending over, panting, and resting his hands on his knees.

"What is it?" I inquire, concerned, jumping into defensive mode. I scan his frazzled features, taking in his rumpled clothing and sweaty forehead.

"One of the fucking men was just caught taking product!" Breathing deeply he hurries on, "I got to him before he could steal any more, but he was able to get out of the building. He ran and escaped out of the east side door. The alarm is off, but we must hurry!"

"Christ, Alexei! You were just in here not even twenty minutes ago! Damn it, find him, Lexei! Now, and return him to me!"

I can't believe these idiots let him get out of the building. I jump up quickly, shoving my chair back and grab my piece out of my desk drawer. You steal from me, the Bratva, it's going to end one way.

I follow Alexei down the hall to the main building. The men are all standing, waiting for orders, and gazing at each other as if it's vodka time. They may as well have their thumbs up their asses.

"Quit standing around and find him!" I roar angrily and they all scatter toward the door.

"You five!" I point toward a group to the left, "Stay and guard the product." I gesture toward the crates wildly and move to the entrance.

Alexei steps close to me, "Boss, please stay and let me handle it."

Turning, I scoff, "You handle it, Alexei?" I snarl, "You were just out here and let him go! You want me to trust you? Then go bring him back!"

I bustle out the door in a fit of irritation. *Just what I wanted to deal with today.* I need to be monitoring the new inventory and making deals, but instead I'm faced with foolishness. Why weren't the doors being watched? Simple tasks yet they can't be done.

Slamming the door behind me, I run outside and around the back of the warehouse to where I hear my men making the most noise. This idiot better hope he can run and find some place to go. There are all types of wildlife out here and I wouldn't be surprised if he didn't survive. He could always go steal a boat off the docks, but I'll be sure to have my guys down there.

There are close to five thousand in the Solntsevskaya Bratva organization together and about thirty who work with me on a regular basis. The majority of the others are delegated through different channels from myself or others I have assigned to certain tasks.

I fly around the corner, ready for just about anything and find four of my guys lugging the thieving idiot roughly back to me. The bum pulls, pushes and fights back trying to get free. Bastard doesn't make it far as they hit him in the stomach and kidneys several times.

It's in his best interest to fight, he knows what's about to come of him. I have a zero tolerance policy for stealing. Watching for a few moments as my men beat him, I smirk. It's the least of his worries.

Approaching them carefully, I attempt to stay out of the way of swinging fists and elbows.

Taking in the surroundings, I cautiously scan for anyone who could be watching. I'm pleased to find that we are indeed alone, as we should be. I picked this location as my main supply building for a reason.

I sneer at him, getting angrier with each step as I approach. "Where was it you planned on going? There is nothing but trees and water, you imbecile! Did you seriously think you would get away with it?"

He shakes his head and spits in my direction.

"Do you have any clue just who I am?" I ask curiously.

This man seriously has a death wish by spitting toward me. That is such a disgraceful sign of disrespect. My uncle would have chopped him into little bits, starting with that nasty tongue of his.

"Nyet," he replies in Russian and shakes his head.

"Ah." I click my tongue. "Shame. I am Viktor Masterson, head of the organization you were working for and are stupid enough to spit at," I reply snidely, glaring at him.

He turns his face away from me and looks in the other direction. This trash has lost his mind if he thinks I will tolerate this behavior in front of my men. I remove my suit jacket and hand it to Sergei, one of my guards. He follows me pretty much everywhere so he's accustomed to being my coat rack when needed.

I unbutton my cuff links and roll up my sleeves leisurely, taking a nice deep breath to clear my lungs. Moving my head side to side to pop my neck muscles and loosen up. I draw my arm back and punch the jackass square in the jaw.

His head flies backwards with the momentum and there's an audible crack that echoes in the trees. "Ugh!" he moans loudly. I'm sure he has a tooth floating around in there now.

Swiftly, I pull out my weapon. Cocking it, I smile and aim it straight in the middle of his forehead. His eyes widen, surprised. I pull the trigger without a moment of hesitation.

He drops like a sack of potatoes and the men stand there holding him. They're all silent, staring at me and waiting. I guess I surprised everyone with that one.

"Let it be known that this was me being gentle on someone who steals from me. I will not show the same compassion to the next person who is caught."

"Boss," Alexei answers and nods, motioning at the other men. The group follow suit and nod as well. I turn on my heel and head back inside to my office.

"Take care of it!" I call out loudly as I walk away and hear them scurry to follow orders.

A few moments later I receive a message from Spartak and it makes the entire evening better.

Spartak: She asks for you
Me: Everything okay?
Spartak: Yes, sir

I can't even fathom the fact that she has finally asked about me. My stomach feels as if it wants to implode. I don't know if that feeling is a blessing or a curse. Spartak will have to update me when she's not working. I can't wait to hear what she said.

I grab the keys to my Jaguar; my heart is beating quickly, excited. It's time for me to head home. Clearly I've had enough excitement for today. I nod to Sergei so he knows I'm leaving.

We make it down the hallway before getting caught by Alexei, "Boss?" He gazes at me, questioning.

"I'm leaving. I have to check on the other warehouse tomorrow, so I will expect you at my house at ten in the morning."

"No problem, sir, I will be there."

"Good, you will stay and look over things?"

"Of course, sir. I'm sorry about earlier."

"Until tomorrow," I say and take my leave.

Sergei and I make our way to the cars. He gets in my Jaguar and starts it while I stay about twenty feet away. He always starts my vehicles for me. You never know when someone may try to get back at the Bratva.

Chapter 3

Elaina

This is the third shift of mine he's missed. It means an additional day with Spartak following me around like he's a puppy. He's pleasant; I'm just finding myself speculating about Vik.

I know Viktor and Tate aren't the greatest of guys, but it makes me wonder what they really do if Vik feels I need someone around me constantly. As each day passes, my curiosity and speculations grow. I'm sure I'm imagining something way more sinister than what it really is, but at this point I'm ready to give Viktor a piece of my mind.

I stroll behind the bar in OO7. Another day, another dollar, I suppose.

Hawk is filling in for the other bartender again. He must be exhausted, poor guy is already the manager at Club Taint. He's one of the best bartenders I've ever worked with. He will make my night a cake walk, thankfully. After the scuffle with the drunk, I haven't been too keen on coming in to work. At least I have some eye candy to look forward to. He's sporting his signature blue mohawk, sexy grin and Chucks. I don't mind being around Hawk; he's friendly and has always been respectful toward me. He's one of the few I don't mind with the pet names. Viktor and my sister are the others I've gotten used to.

"Hey, beautiful," he murmurs in his killer raspy voice.

"Hey, you, how's life?"

"It's good, just having woman issues."

"Uh oh, anything I can help with?" I lean my hip against the beer cooler and cross my arms.

"Well, I met this chick, total babe, bright red hair, killer smile and body. She brings food to my shifts a lot but every time I think we are going somewhere, a groupie comes up and fucks it all up. Now Dillian, that's her name, is pissed and is backing off again."

Hawk is a drummer in a rock band when he has spare time. He has some great arms to prove it too. His brother is the singer of the group; I can only imagine his voice with how great Hawk's is. I wonder what the rest of the band looks like.

"That sucks! Have you told the groupies to back off and explained to Dillian that you aren't interested in them?"

A stool scrapes loudly and I glance back to see what Spartak is doing, only I'm met with annoyed green-hazel eyes and a scowl to match.

Viktor looks at Hawk angrily. "Correct me if I'm wrong, but you're supposed to be doing inventory, yes?" It's not really a question, just formed like one. It's more like an annoyed growl.

Hawk nods. "Yeah, I was just on my way to do that."

"Very good," Viktor replies shortly and Hawk walks quickly to the storage room. I put my hand on my hip and spin to face Viktor fully.

"Well, hello, grouchy pants. Why aren't you friendly with Hawk? He's a nice guy."

"He's not my friend, he's my employee. I pay him to work." He shrugs indifferently.

"Well, you also pay me to work, but yet you never seem to have an issue with me talking to you."

"That's entirely different, Elaina," he murmurs, running his hands through his hair.

"Really? How so?" I lean on my elbows against the bar, closer to him. He copies me and leans in closer.

"He's a single man."

"Annnd you're not?"

He grasps my wrists tightly in each of his hands and I draw in a startled gasp. He leans in close and his breath washes over me. I clench, turned on at the sensation.

"No, Printsyessa (Princess), last time I checked, I was all about you."

I tear my hands away and step back. "Uh, Viktor, you're wrong," I reply quietly.

I pace toward the end of the bar and busy myself. I bow down and start shifting glasses around into straight rows. I get nervous and it causes me to act as if I have ADD.

Regardless of feeling a presence behind me, I stay bent over. It's one of those moments where you clench your tummy tightly and lie, telling yourself nothing's behind you when in fact you know there really is something there.

I'm startled when a strong hand grasps my bicep, pulling me up and backward. I spin, ready to fight and let loose a piece of my mind. I'm met with Viktor's serious expression about four inches from my face and it makes me pause, forgetting every word that had been wanting to come out.

"NO. You are wrong. I have been chasing you for *months*. Open your eyes." He steps closer so I can feel his warm, sweet breath whisper over my face each time he speaks. "Printsyessa," he whispers and tenderly takes my bottom lip between his. My pussy throbs wantonly at his touch.

Freezing up, I open my eyes wide, chanting inside not to freak out. He pulls back, releasing my lip from his. His hand brushes my cheek gently and I feel his breath as he pants close to my lips. I can taste each breath of his I breathe in. I open my lips slightly, my mouth watering at the idea of his being so close to mine.

"Viktor," I choke and he dives in roughly, ravaging my mouth as if he is starving and I can quench his hunger. One hand grasps my cheek and the other rests on the bar behind me as he forcefully pushes my body against it with his.

His body is hard, demanding, and wanting. I tightly grasp his shirt as I let him take my mouth. His tongue caresses mine, teaching me how to please him.

His hand leaves my face and trails up my thigh under my skirt. It's like a splash of cold water and I push him away forcefully.

Panting, I step to the side and press my hand to my swollen lips. "I'm sorry, but I just can't," I say, ashamed. Why does there have to be something wrong with me? Why can't I just be like everyone else?

"You can't now, but you will," he says sternly and walks away from me.

I stand still holding my mouth and shake my head. My skin is sensitive to the touch from his five o'clock shadow. God, I wish I could give him what he wants, but it will never happen. I watch him walk down the hall and to the office. *Just great, what am I going to do now?*

I attempt to make the night pass quickly by being diligent and extra friendly to the customers I get. It just doesn't work, Hawk asks me like twenty times to tell him what is eating at me, but I'm not someone who opens up. I learned many years ago to hold it all inside.

I guess my sister and I have more in common than I realized. I like to keep stuff to myself and she is stubborn, always trying to do everything by herself. We are twins, so I guess we are bound to have things in common.

I know one thing; I will never forgive myself for hitting her with my car, but I'm torn, Had I not been drinking and driving I never would have found her in the first place since I had no clue she even existed. Yet I always end up beating myself up because I could have killed my only family member. I could have killed her before I ever had the chance to know about her.

Thank God she ended up being okay without serious injuries. Now she's giving me more family with her baby. She's had nothing but struggle in her life. I deserve every ounce of pain I received from that damn wreck.

Viktor eventually makes his way back out sometime during my shift. I am busy making another tray of martinis and when I turn around, notice him sitting in his usual spot. He doesn't say anything; he's being his normal quiet self and glaring at any guy who looks at me for too long. I never would have pegged him for the jealous type. After the endless refills of martinis I've made this shift, I could do with never making one again.

The club is brimming with thug-like guys tonight for some reason. I don't know what is going on, but Viktor chewed out his guard, Alexei, earlier. He looked so angry I thought he was going to strangle him. I don't like seeing his guard getting in trouble, but have to admit seeing Viktor with so much power draws me to him.

I'm busy finishing up my closing duties. I always have the early shift doing the prep work, so I get to leave earlier than the others. Grabbing my things, I notice a chick approach Viktor. She's all skanked up in a short dress and a pound of make-up. I suppose men probably find her pretty, whereas I like a more natural look. Viktor watches me as she whispers in his ear, giggling like a hyena.

Whatever, I don't have time for that. I roll my eyes and grab my soda in my Styrofoam to-go cup. I walk from behind the bar and he stands up, brushing off the girl and quickly makes his way to me.

The woman glares spitefully when she sees him come to my side. I'm not a hateful person but I can't help the smirk that appears on my face as we pass her by. My stomach flutters with excitement at the prospect of someone believing he's my man.

She steps in front of me with her hands on her hips, wearing a snotty expression. She obviously thinks she has something important to say.

Stopping abruptly, I look at her like she's lost her mind. She's crazy to just pop in front of people as they are walking, we could have run right into her. I have a feeling I'm not going to want to hear whatever she plans to say.

Viktor places his arm in front of me, pushing me back slightly and I shoot him a peeved look. He ignores it and commands the female's full attention just by his strong presence. His back muscles stiffen under his suit jacket as he stands in front of me.

"Get out of the way, Kendall," he says sternly, looking at her in irritation and demanding her immediate compliance.

She continues to poke her head around him and glare at me hatefully. My blood boils as I realize something; she has no valid reason to act this way toward me. I've had my fill of the ugly looks I get from people.

I push against his arm and get up close to her, right in her face. I may not like a man touching me, but after growing up in a few foster facilities, I've learned how to hold my own with a female. This is no exception; you put chicks in their place right away or you'll have issues with them forever.

"Can I help you?" I inquire, staring her down and flaring my nostrils.

Scrunching up her pointy nose, she sneers, "Uh yeah, I wasn't done talking to Viktor." I swear, I could just grab her nose and give it a good twist. I can't stand women who act like this. They think they're so entitled, when in reality, no one owes them shit. She's got a bad case of too many handouts.

I splay my hand beside me dramatically like I'm introducing the President or something. "Have at it then, sweetie pie."

I turn to Viktor and he shakes his head.

I glance back at her, wide eyed. "Well, Kendaall, guess you have your answer, huh."

I tend to draw my words out when I'm being sarcastic. It's a bad habit, but I can't seem to shake it plus it drives people crazy when I do it. I'm betting it will grate on her nerves also.

"Ugh!" She yells and shoves me backwards.

Yeah, I don't think so, bitch. I shove her back and she comes at me. Grabbing her shoulders, I head butt her in her pointy nose without hesitation. *That will definitely need surgery to look perfect again.* I'm not about to let her get a hit in, I've learned about that the hard way. Blood sprays from the gash and her nose bleeds heavily.

She shrieks and I can't help but snicker a little. Call it payback from some of us less entitled folks. People start pointing and surrounding us, ready to watch a fight. They're too late though, I know she won't bounce back from a hit like that.

Viktor gapes at me, surprised and maybe even a little impressed. He yanks me forcefully toward the back door, shouting for Sergei to grab the other girl. I'm sucked into the chaos and shouting; it feels like we're leaving the club. Everyone's voices melt together and I start to feel a little dizzy from the adrenaline rush.

I glance down to make sure I still have my stuff and notice I have blood sprayed all over the front of me. I have little drops all over my arm and shirt. Well, Emily's shirt. *Shit.* This is another reason why I don't buy nice clothes, well, besides not really being able to afford them.

"Come on, you little troublemaker," Viktor says loudly, threading our fingers together and pulling me through the throng of people.

We head out the back door toward the alley where he always keeps his vehicle parked. Sure enough, his car is there waiting with Spartak driving. How convenient.

"Wait, I have to get my car." I pull back from his grasp, slightly resisting but he holds on.

"No, Elaina, come on, just get in. I'll bring you back to get your car later. Curious people will start coming out that door, and we need to be gone. Things could turn very ugly and I refuse to submit you to that."

Spartak jumps out of the driver's seat quickly to open the back door and Viktor rushes me inside. I slide to the rear passenger side and he scoots in beside me.

"Go, Spar," Viktor orders and Spartak speeds away efficiently.

"Why are you in such a hurry? It was just a little blood." I glance at him curiously. From the way he acts in the bar I thought he was a bad ass.

"Yeah, it was just a little bit of blood you took from an important man's daughter. Christ, I'm pretty confident you broke her nose back there."

I open my mouth to respond and defend myself but he holds his hand up, signaling that he needs one minute. He pulls his phone out and quickly dials a number. I eaves drop the best I can.

"Alexei, have you left?"

"Okay, when you leave, call her father and schedule a meeting, offer my apologies."

He presses end and places his phone in his inside jacket pocket. The whole inside is lined in what appears to be silk or some other delicate material.

I sit still, staring at him and he turns to me, giving me his attention again. I wish I could have heard what Alexei was saying on the other end. It's the club's fault with all the loud music, my ears are still ringing.

"You may finish now," he says and reaches across me to grab my seatbelt. My heart quickens as he stretches it across me and buckles it. "Just like your sister," he murmurs and sends me a chastising look. "Tate always tells me that he has to buckle her in." He shakes his head again and smirks at me. I roll my eyes in defiance.

"I'm honored to be like my sister, she's a good person."

"I know she is. That poor girl has been through a lot. She will make a fantastic, strong mother."

"I know! I can't wait to be an aunty!" I grin excitedly. "I'm going to have the baby call me Tanta."

"I did not know you were German, you strike me closer to Russian."

"I don't know if I'm German or not, I just think it sounds cool. I haven't talked to Emily much about that part of our lives. Is that why you like me, because I look Russian?"

He shrugs and sits back in his seat a little. The smooth leather seats are out-of-this-world comfortable. I hope he doesn't just like me for my looks. That Kendall chick was pretty in her own face-painted-like-a-clown way.

"Who says I like you at all, Printsyessa (Princess)?"

"Well, the stalking factor sort of clues me in."

He chuckles loudly. "Stalking, huh? Is that what you call it? I call it looking out for you. Kind of like a guardian angel. Yes, think of me as an angel."

"An angel? Yeaaaah right." I smile cheekily and wink.

"I know. I am not a particularly good man, maybe a dark angel. Nonetheless, I will care for you."

"But why, Viktor? I don't get it. Why would you care about me in the first place? It's been so long and you've gotten nothing from me. A failed date and some not so interesting family dinners with my sister, Tate, and myself. I don't understand why you would still be giving me the time of day and not moving onto someone else by now."

I swallow deeply as he lightly runs his pointer finger along my skirt hem next to my thigh. He scoots back in; close enough to me that I can see the stress lines next to his eyes. My tummy flips over and over as I try to concentrate on not moving my leg away from him.

"You are wrong, you give me everything."

"What could I possibly give you?" I mutter in a disbelieving voice, studying his beautiful eyes.

"I'll settle for your heart," he purrs and smiles devilishly.

"Good luck with that one, bud." I chortle, raising my eyebrows and he laughs again. I always see him stressed and serious, it's nice that when he's around me he can relax and laugh. In fact, he always laughs and smiles a lot when we are together for lunch or whatever. I get all warm inside knowing that, I love it.

"Are you hungry?"

"No, not really, but I do need to go to my car."

"All right if you insist. Spartak, please take us to her car."

"Yes, sir."

Spartak turns the car around and makes the short, uneventful drive to the employee area where my car is. I love being around Viktor but I don't think I can handle it if he keeps playing with my skirt. My nerves are bouncing all over the place.

I start to reach for the door handle, ready to jump out as soon as we stop.

"Wait." Viktor voice is husky as he gently grabs my wrist. I glance down at his hand and he follows suit. I snatch my wrist out of his grasp and he looks at me, puzzled. Spartak opens my door and I quickly unbuckle, moving to get out.

Viktor grabs me again. I turn quickly to correct him, only I'm met with his mouth on mine before I even have a chance to process what's happening. I'm pulled to him so my shoulder and part of my breast are firmly resting against his strong chest.

Grasping my face, he keeps it turned to him so he can ravish me as he pleases. Returning his kiss fervently, I pour out all of my pent up frustration and aggression into the kiss. My stomach melts inside as his tongue thoroughly caresses mine.

Viktor gradually pulls away, kissing my top and bottom lips softly, chastely. I remain still, unmoving, relishing in the feeling of being touched and kissed and actually enjoying it.

He tenderly places his forehead on the side of mine, holding my face in place, and I keep my eyes closed. *Just enjoy this feeling a little longer.*

He whispers gruffly, "Now that – that is how our kiss should have been."

Vik places a tender kiss in my hair and I pull back. I look him in the eyes and nod minutely, staying silent. He literally took my breath away just now. My mind is reeling trying to process this feeling of wanting to do more right now instead of being scared as I normally would be.

Grasping my purse, I scramble out of the vehicle quickly and he lets me go. I was almost expecting him to hold me back. Maybe pull me in and kiss me again. Perhaps that's just what I wish would happen.

Turning to face him, I stand beside the car, peering at him dazedly. I take in his dilated eyes, chest rising rapidly and clenched fists making him appear even more delicious. I lean in, kindly saying, "Thank you for caring about me, Viktor."

"Good night, my lovely," he responds and grins as Spartak closes the car door and leads me to my vehicle. Minus the scuffle in the club, I'd say it was an exceptionally good night.

41

Chapter 4

Viktor
One week later...

I'm standing in the club chatting with Alexei about business when he immediately moves in front of me to intercept Nikoli. Niko's my brother's pet, the blond gorilla, who is storming toward me at full speed.

He would probably smash Alexei up quite easily, but my guards are loyal. They will take it as much as possible in order to protect me. I can't imagine what could possibly have Niko wound up in a tizzy, to come at me like this.

"It's okay, Alexei, he's Tate's man." I tap him lightly on the shoulder and he moves back to my side.

Niko yells loudly, his Russian accent stronger than mine, as he shoves in to me "You fuck!"

Backing up, I place my hands up in a placating gesture and breathe deeply, attempting to cool my rising temper before I do something to upset my little brother. Niko obviously has a death wish, pushing me like that.

"Nikoli! Touch me again and I will put you in a lake!" I growl sternly and he huffs angrily in return. "Did you jump Tate's leash? He would have your head if he were to witness your behavior right now."

"I am on no leash, ass face. Tate is my best friend, he would show me support." His outburst is defensive.

"No, you are his guard, Nikoli, and you are messing with business and family right now. Tell me, why are you wasting my time and why am I not drowning you right now?"

"Do you have any clue who Kendall is?"

"Of course I do, I have had business with her father in the past."

"Well, I hear from her sister you bust her nose. Bina not happy so I come to fix."

"I did not bust that troll's face. She was interfering with Elaina and me leaving the club. She started it and Elaina finished it. I spoke to her father the other day and everything is settled."

42

"How is it settled? I have not heard of this."

"He asked me to take her to lunch and apologize. I agreed. Not that it's your business. Who is Bina?"

"Sabrina Cheslokov, Kendall's younger sister."

"Ahh, I see, and you fancy her?"

He looks at me skeptically. "She is good friend."

"Very well. I understand. Is that all?"

"Yes, my apologies, sir, I didn't know it was fixed."

"I understand that." He starts to turn around. "Oh and Nikoli?" I call out calmly and he turns back to me.

"The next time you want to inquire, have my brother call. You approach me in such a manner again, and I will not hesitate to teach you manners. You forget my brother is not the only powerful man around here."

He looks taken aback for a moment then nods in resignation. "Sir," he says and when I nod back he takes his leave.

"You okay, Boss?" Alexei turns to me, concerned.

He scans me from head to toe once Niko is out of the club. I pull on my jacket to straighten it out again, brushing the small creases with my hands. I can't stand not looking professional when I'm out in public.

"I'm fine," I grunt. "I'll let that one go." I rub my temples, trying to soothe my irritation, and continue, "I know what it feels like to be taken with someone and wanting vengeance when they are hurt."

"Are you planning on letting Knees know about what happened?"

"No, I know if I call my brother he will put Niko down and I don't want to take his close friend from him. Don't call him that in public either. That name is for our ears only and I don't want the wrong person getting wind of it. There are many Feds out there trying to figure out who matches up with that name."

"Yes, sir, of course. It won't happen again," he responds and goes back to watching the club.

"Would you like anything, Viktor?" my Printsyessa asks, distracting me from my anger.

Smiling slightly at the light she ignites inside me each time I hear her voice, I gaze at her, entranced by her stunning blue eyes. "No, lovely, I'm fine. I need to go handle a few things. Are you okay? I will leave Spartak for you."

"I understand you can't always be here, Viktor, and it's okay. Thank you for always hanging out, but go. I'll be okay and you don't have to leave Spartak if you need him."

"No, Elaina, I will leave him. I like knowing someone is here to help if you need anything. It gives me peace of mind and calms me."

"Okay, if you insist. I'm going to pretend he's my personal assistant though, less of a stalker feeling. I have to go sit in on a meeting, so I'll see you later?"

"Of course, you can see me anytime you wish." She blushes and I grin in response. "Shall we have dinner?"

"I guess that would be fine, but nothing crazy. Just something simple, please."

"I promise I'll keep it tame." I had tried to wow her in the past and it was the opposite, she left and went home prior to even eating. I was embarrassed to say the least and haven't had the nerve to ask her for another chance until now.

"Okay, great," she replies with a beautiful bright smile.

Finally she agrees to dinner with me again. It's been months and this time I'm not screwing my chance up. Now I just have to figure out something she will like. I wish I didn't have to leave her right now.

It's Saturday morning, around eleven, and Elaina has to go to that boring staff meeting she mentioned. Then she'll be stuck here doing the weekend prep for the staff. She's off but comes in to get paid for a few hours of prep and stocking.

I came up with it so she would have an easy way to make the extra money I know she needs. She isn't aware that it's not a normal position and I prefer it that way. I wanted to pay her even more but the manager said it would be too obvious. The other bartenders were happy to give up some of their required side work. They are lazy goons wanting to slack off, nothing like my sweet Elaina.

Unfortunately, I have to meet with Kendall today for our 'lunch date'. I don't want to, but I am keen on keeping the peace between our families. The best part about today will be getting to have dinner with Elaina. It will completely make up for having to subject myself to Kendall for an hour or so.

Elaina

I'm sitting through this mind-numbing meeting listening to the manager basically telling us all how we are doing a shitty job and to quit slacking off. I work my butt off here so I'm pretty much ignoring him. As if dealing with the drunk assholes isn't enough, the manager has to be one too.

I stare, bored, at his bald little head and beady gaze. I don't understand how he even has this position. I wonder if he's related to the Masterson's and they just gave him the spot. I could do a better job with this place than he does. Aren't managers supposed to interact with customers and motivate their employees? Because we get none of that with him.

My phone beeps loudly with an alert in the quiet room and everyone in the meeting turns to me. *Shit!* I forgot to turn it on silent. I always do that and hate when this happens! Todd, the asshole manager, grunts, and stares at me, irritated.

"Umm, sorry," I stammer. *Fuck!*

He shakes his head and turns back to resume talking. I roll my eyes defiantly; that idiot just makes me want to throat punch him, he's such a jerk. I'd bet your sweet ass his phone isn't on silent either.

Might as well check it out since everyone knows it went off anyhow. I swipe my finger across the screen and a new message pops up from an unknown number. I click on the message to download the attachment.

A few beats later after it finishes loading I'm staring at an image of Viktor and that snotty bitch from the other night.

Kendall's dressed to the nines. All slutted up in a snakeskin print dress that dips so low down her chest her breasts would be showing in a strong gust of wind. She probably weighs an extra ten pounds with her obnoxious jewelry. Her painted on face is bright with laughter, and Viktor's smirking. They're seated in what appears to be a fancy restaurant and Kendall's arm is stretched across the table, resting on his wrist.

My anger swells up into my throat. I study Kendall's features closely, I'm glad to see her nose still looks bruised. *Ugh! Stupid bitch!* I know Viktor's not mine, but he's here for me almost every shift! Does this mean he sees her during the day? Then shows up here in the evening? I tell him nothing fancy, so he takes her to a nice place instead. Viktor has nerve to spew that shit about caring for me and then take Kendall to lunch.

He can go fuck a duck. I'm not meeting his ass for dinner. Fuck that shit. I look at the number again. I don't recognize it; I'm going to text it back.

Me: Who is this?
Unknown: No one
Me: Why did you send this?
Unknown: You should know the Devil you spend time with
Me: Devil?
Me: Why is he a Devil?
Me: Hello?

I get no response and I feel my throat wanting to close up on me as if I've just been stung by a thousand bees. I stand abruptly in the middle of the meeting, "Fuck this." I choke the words out loudly and walk out.

Todd stands there with his mouth open, gaping at me. I don't care, won't be the first time I walked out of a place and probably won't be the last. I'm sick of these Russians.

I hurry to my car in the employee parking area. Slamming the door and revving the engine, I peel out through the gravel parking lot, spewing rocks all over Viktor's car that the guard uses and grinning manically as it happens.

Good, fuck that dude. I start to pass the liquor barn and flip a U-turn to go through the drive-thru. It dings loudly when I pull up to the window.

"Can I help you, ma'am?" I start to reply *vodka* and gag on my words.

No vodka and no Russians.

"Tequila. Give me a pint of José Silver, a pint of cheap rum and a two liter of Coke."

The dorky kid sniffs and nods. "Sure, just a sec." I wait impatiently, drumming my fingers on the steering wheel. "That'll be twenty-four dollars and fifty-one cents please."

I hand the guy twenty-five dollars. "Keep the change." I gesture to him, indifferent. He beams, showing off his acne-decorated cheeks and hands me my paper bag full of liquid pain killers.

I pull up in the parking lot and pour about a quarter of the Coke out my window onto the ground, then dump the pint of rum in it. Screwing the lid on tightly, I turn it upside down carefully, then back upright and rest the bottle between my legs for when I'm ready. I twist open the cap on the tequila and place it next to me in the cup holder, perfect for easy access.

Rolling my window back up, I take a large swig of tequila, swiftly chasing the tequila shot with my soda/rum mixture. It burns my throat and chest, but I delight in the feeling, knowing it will steal away my thoughts from me soon.

Hammering down on the gas, I head to my apartment. My poor Camaro's taking a beating today but I don't want to have a repeat of when I crashed my car. It's amazing that I'm even allowed to drive.

If it weren't for Tate's lawyers I would have spent time in jail, paid a hefty fee and lost my license. I almost killed them. Tate got me off with a lot of cash. It's just something else to beat myself up about while I drink myself into a stupor.

I take another large gulp of my rum, swerving as I hold the big bottle. Pulling swiftly into my parking spot I'm surprised when hear a screech of tires. Glancing in the rear view mirror, I see Spartak's black car parked behind me, effectively blocking me in.

He jumps out in haste as soon as he slams the car in park, rushing to my window. Spartak beats angrily on the glass with his fist, glaring at me. I unlock the door and stagger out leisurely.

Spartak bellows, "Have you lost your mind?! Viktor will KILL me if something happens to you! What was that back there?" He's too close so I shove against him to back off some.

"Yeah right! Viktor doesn't give a shit!" I shout back at Spar and round the car to get my purse and bottles.

"You've completely lost it, woman, he follows you around like a lovesick fool. You're the only person he cares for besides his family, the only one he's even remotely nice to."

"Is that so? Then why would he be seeing *her*?" I ask, the liquor starting to thrum through me.

He peers at me, bewildered, as if he doesn't have a clue what I'm talking about. "Pshh, whatever, it's not even worth it." I shoo him with my hand. Snatching up my things angrily, I take a swig of tequila and head to my apartment. Spartak stands next to my car, staring at me, worried.

I make it into my apartment, slam the door and lock the crappy locks. Screw them all, I'm going to forget about all men, about all of my problems.

I chug my soda mixture and love the dizziness that starts to show up to overtake my mind.

Viktor

My phone vibrates and I check it immediately. Deep inside I hope it's Elaina. She's the only one I ever want it to be.

Spartak: I don't know what happened, Boss. She's drinking and upset. She almost wrecked driving crazy. I'm at her apartment but locked out.

My heart speeds erratically as I read the message. What on earth happened? Elaina was just fine. God, I hope she's okay. I can't listen to this twat for a second longer, my princess needs me.

Clearing my throat loudly, I lean forward. "Please excuse me, Kendall, an emergency has come up. Sergei will finish out lunch with you, I am truly sorry." She shoots me a look mixed between worry and pouty.

"Oh no, okay, Viktor, I understand. Go, baby, and we can finish up another time. You will be missed badly," she replies in her whiny voice. God, Kendall disgusts me. She's so pretentious; I could never care for her no matter how much her father wants me to.

"Thank you for understanding," I answer and nod at Sergei. I'm just not interested in being here. I speedily make my way to the valet and give him my ticket. I slip him a hundred.

"Quickly, please."

He nods. "My pleasure, sir."

The valet rushes off and a few seconds later my Mercedes approaches. I get in swiftly and lay on the gas. She screeches on the smooth surface and I'm off like a rocket. I turn up the radar detector volume and get to Elaina's hole-in-the-wall as quickly as I can.

As I park next to Elaina's car and my sedan, I see Spar standing outside. He's leaning against her wall next to the door looking pale. Music is pouring out from her place.

I hustle out, slamming my door. "What's that?" I gesture to Elaina's door.

"I think it's called '*Superman*' by an artist called Eminem. She's had it on repeat, so I Googled it."

"No, not the song, idiot, what's going on with her? What's the mess?"

"I don't know, sir. When she arrived she was drinking and talking about you not caring for her. I knocked after she went in, but she won't answer."

He looks distraught. It appears he has also come to care for her, probably from me having him always watching her. I'm glad; it means he will protect her better. On the downside, if he gets too close to her, I will have him put down.

I look up at the sky, exasperated. "Of course I care for Elaina, have you tried the door?"

"Yes, Boss, it's locked."

I nod and pound on her door a few times. I get no answer so I remove my jacket, hand it to Spartak and roll up my sleeves. I pull my pants legs up slightly and kick forcefully next to the locks.

The door splinters next to the lock, from the crappy quality. I kick once more and the door goes flying open. The music loudly thrums around me as I scan the living area. *God, I can only imagine what she's thinking while listening to this song, over and over.*

I find her in the kitchen, sitting at her table. She has her arms resting on the plastic surface with her head in her hands, gripping her hair tightly. Her shoulders shake: she appears so fragile, almost broken.

"Have you gone mad?" I boom.

She's surrounded by an empty rum bottle, a large soda, and a tequila bottle that's about a quarter gone. Elaina freezes in her trembling and slowly glances up at me as if she doesn't believe she heard my voice.

"Well?" I bellow and gesture around me at her trashed apartment.

She glares crossly at me, spearing me with her gaze. Her face is swollen and she has hot tears running down her cheeks.

"What do you care, Viktor? Go back to your priorities," Elaina responds heatedly.

She's not fragile after all, broken maybe, but she's definitely ready for a fight.

"You are my priority, Printsyessa"

"LIAR!" she screams and throws the empty rum bottle at me. I duck to the side. She would have clipped me with the bottle had I not moved so quickly. This is new; I've seen her upset, but she's ready to castrate me.

"I do not lie! Stop this nonsense and talk to me!"

Elaina jumps up quickly, roars and charges at me. She goes ballistic, beating on my chest, and I let her. "Ugh! I hate you!" she screams.

Rearing back she punches me violently in my chin. My temper ignites and I slap her. Not hard but enough to get her attention. I clench my hands into fists, trying to reel in my anger. The last thing I want to do is cause her any harm, but I won't stand for her hitting me like that.

"You hit me as a man, Printsyessa, I will hit you back! Now pull yourself together, Elaina! Enough of this. You want to talk, then tell me what this craziness is about and I will fix it."

She drops her hands and buries her face into my chest, sobbing. She's had way too much to drink and it's amplifying her anger.

"Please, lovely, tell me what is hurting you?" I ask, burying my nose into her hair.

The music stops and I glance over to see Spartak. He looks at me anxiously and leaves, closing the broken front door behind him.

"Please, my love, speak," I murmur in Russian.

She gasps, choking out, "You were with her and I just couldn't take it anymore. All men do is hurt me, and I just couldn't take it."

"With whom?" I clasp her chin gently, tilting her face up to mine.

"The bitch from last week who I hit."

"Ahh, Kendall. I was at lunch trying to apologize. Her father is a powerful man and I was trying to keep peace, that's all. You thought I was seeing her?"

"Yea-yes, I mean the picture looked like it was more."

"Picture? You got a picture? Show me."

Elaina pulls her phone from her back pocket and hands it to me. I turn on the screen and the first thing that appears is a photo of me about an hour ago. Elaina's right, it does look like an intimate date between lovers.

"No, no, no, you are wrong. It really isn't how it looks. I am so sorry. I was telling her about my brother's friend coming to her defense and she was laughing. Kendall's fake, she is absolutely nothing to me. Elaina, if there is anyone, it is only you. I swear it." After this conversation is over, I'm finding out who the hell took that photograph.

She leans back, looking at me for the first time like I'm not some evil creature set out to destroy her.

"You really care about me?"

"Of course I do, I've only been telling you this for months. However, I'm curious as to what you meant by men hurting you. Please elaborate."

Elaina's expression shutters and she shakes her head. "It's nothing. I was just upset. God, I can't believe I punched you. I'm so sorry."

"It's not a big deal; after seeing the picture I can understand why you were so angry." She nods, chewing on her lip.

Murmuring close to her ear, I ask, "Is it sick of me to think you look absolutely beautiful right now?"

She shakes her head and looks at the ground. I tip her face back up toward mine. After that fight, I'm spinning with need.

Bending slightly, I grab the outsides of her thighs, picking her up, and I wrap her strong legs around me. Elaina peers at me, taken aback for a moment before she leans in and kisses me passionately.

Eagerly I return her kiss, as I carry her to the couch. After stooping down and laying her gently on the squeaky furniture, I rest on top of her, trying not to squish her, and kiss her fervently.

I weave my hand in her silky blonde locks, clutching them tightly and pull her head back, exposing her neck. I lick and kiss, sucking, nibbling on her throat, getting lost a little more with each one.

Elaina squirms underneath and I thrust my hardness against her. Each little movement sends a powerful stroke of pleasure surging through my anatomy. It envelops me with need, causing my body to vibrate with hunger.

"Oh, Viktor, I want, I want," Elaina pants, breathless.

"Yes, Princess," I mumble and thrust against her again.

I grind my cock in a circle motion and she calls out loudly. I use my other hand to grasp onto her breast, lightly pinching her pebbled peak through her thin shirt and bra.

"Oh please," she begs and I push her shirt up quickly. I pull her breasts out of her bra, exposing sweet little peach nipples.

I grind my hardness into her again and she gazes at me with flames in her eyes. Elaina's so turned on she looks as if she would burn up. The only thing separating us are her little panties and my pants. I push her skirt up higher so I can get to the top of her cotton panties.

"Sweet, sweet, Princess." I groan as I rub her clit tenderly. She throws her head back, face and neck flushing. She looks astounding.

"Oh, Viktor, that feels so, so good."

I use my free hand to pull my cock out while rubbing her. She has her eyes closed so she doesn't notice. I slide her panties to the side. Her bare sex glistens with wetness and my cock throbs with want. *Yes.*

I place my tip to her opening and her eyes snap wide open, staring at me as I thrust forcefully into her extremely tight little hole.

"Ahhh, OH!" she yells and clutches onto my shoulders tightly.

Wow, she may be the tightest woman I've ever been with. I push in again slowly as her tender pussy squeezes me snugly, burying myself to the hilt. She gasps and a tear escapes.

I kiss it away and purr, "Shh, Princess, it's okay. This is how it's supposed to be, just you and me. You feel amazing."

"Viktor, I... I haven't." I interrupt her and kiss her soundly. I don't want to hear excuses or anything else. I just want to lose myself in her.

After a few beats Elaina relents, relaxing her muscles. She's still extremely tight but at least it's not painful to move anymore. She gets a little wetter and I bend her knee up, driving deeply. I feel each little squeeze her pussy makes and in return I pant, attempting to hold back from pounding her too roughly.

"Yes," she groans quietly and stares into my eyes with each full plunge.

I use my free hand to capture hers and pin them on the arm of the couch behind her head. Gripping her wrists tightly, I drive my dick in quicker, thoroughly lubricating it in her juices. *I'm going to make sure every piece of her remembers this moment.*

"You're so perfect," I whisper against her mouth, kissing her lips.

She makes little moans as her pussy drips, her wetness coating my cock and testicles. I move my hips in circles spreading her essence, grinding into her and stimulating her clit.

"Oh! It's feeling even better!" Elaina pants, gasping in pleasure and I feel the first strong pulses of her pussy starting to orgasm.

I suck strongly on her round peach peak, making it stiffen further. Her cunt spasms erratically, her walls clutch me fiercely and push me over the edge. I can't help myself; I drive into her forcefully a few times, gripping Elaina's thigh tightly. I know there will be bruises left but I can't stop, she feels too good. My dick throbs, pouring my cum so completely inside her.

"Oh, my love." I grunt in bliss, completely sated, kissing her neck and cheek.

It takes a minute until I realize she's stiff as a board underneath me. Glancing down at her, Elaina appears as if she's seen a ghost. "What is it?" I ask kindly.

"Please, move," she whispers, lip trembling and her eyes pooling with water again. *What did I do now?*

"Alright, am I too heavy?" I grin at her, trying to lighten the mood. It just went from great to awful. She shakes her head and I climb off, puzzled.

Elaina glances at my cock and I stand proudly for her to admire my length. I know I'm not a small man and I'm proud of that fact. Her lip trembles again when she looks at it.

She scrambles up and walks to her room. I glance down at my cock, confused. He didn't do anything wrong, in fact Elaina seemed to really enjoy him for a while.

I don't understand why she's upset now. I thought we were past it. Only my cock isn't just coated in wetness and cum, but a little blood as well. *No way.*

Glancing up after her, I call down her small hallway, "Come here, Elaina."

"Please just leave. I don't want to talk anymore." Her declaration is shaky.

"Oh no, Princess, we are talking about this."

"I said just go, damn it! You got what you wanted, now leave."

I make my way down the hallway and stand in the doorway. Elaina's in her shoebox-sized bathroom, turning on the shower. I push my pants the rest of the way off and unbutton my shirt.

She's not going to get in that shower and wash me off her completely. I'll get in there with her so she can't try to forget what just happened. Elaina climbs in and after my shirt's off, I climb in with her.

She shrieks a little when she sees me. I guess she wasn't expecting me to climb in here. She's mad if she thinks I would just up and disappear.

"What are you doing in here? I told you to leave!"

"I'm not leaving you, I just took you, and it means you're mine now. You're mistaken if you thought I would leave after something so important happening. I may be cruel but I will never treat you that way."

"Important? What's important?" she asks stubbornly, snatching up her loofah and dumping Caress soap all over it. It's a tan color and smells sweet like her skin did earlier.

"Elaina, I am not ignorant. I know I just took your virginity."

Tears start to rain down her cheeks. They mingle with the shower spray and she turns away from me. She scrubs harshly at her arms with her pink poof.

"Please, you will harm yourself," I say and clutch her arm softly, attempting to stop her. I take the loofah from her and begin to run it over her back delicately, cleaning her while she silently cries. It hurts me inside to see her so upset and all I can think about is how to fix what's eating at her.

"Please open up to me, I promise I will try to help with whatever is going through your mind right now." I put soap in my hands and

54

gently massage her tense shoulders. I rub deep circles into the muscles, then up and down lightly.

Elaina leans her forehead against the white tile shower wall as she sobs. "You would never understand, Viktor."

"I might understand more than you can fathom; try me."

"I just have a thing with touching," she utters quietly and my hands stiffen. I spin her around carefully to face me and study her face closely.

"What do you mean, with touching, exactly? Please elaborate a little."

She picks at her purple nail polish and stammers, "I don't-don't normally like to be touched. Now when you touch me, I crave it and I don't understand why. I have never wanted a man to touch me like I do you."

"Tell me, why were you never touched? Why was such a beauty as yourself, still a virgin?" I hold her shoulders tightly and look at her with genuine concern. She looks to the ground, tapping her fingers against her thighs and shakes her head.

After a short pause she chokes brokenly, "I'm dirty, Viktor," and I catch my breath.

She winces then brings her blue irises to meet mine. "I was touched too much before. I know you would never want someone who's so fucked up and I don't blame you," she murmurs. "I'm just so glad it was you and not him." She starts to sob again.

I remove my hands and tip her chin up to me.

"There is nothing dirty about you. You, sweet princess, are pure. You're kind, helpful, caring, and beautiful. There is nothing sullied about you. You're telling me someone touched you wrongly?" Anger clouds my gaze.

Elaina nods slightly, bringing her fingers to her lips, upset and I lose it, punching the shower wall wildly. "Give me a name!" I roar.

"It was nobody. Please just forget I told you, I try to forget."

"A name, NOW!" I am furious.

She nods slightly, looking at the floor again, and whispers, "My foster father, Brent Tollfree. It was years ago, I'm okay now."

"Okay? This is not okay! Tollfree? Brent Tollfree – he has short brown hair and is about this tall?" I hold my hand up and she looks at me, perplexed.

She nods. "Yes. You know him?" she hisses, eyes widening in horror.

"Oh, don't you worry about Tollfree ever again. I will take care of this immediately."

"No! Viktor, you can't! You will get in trouble, please, he's a mean man. Just leave it, I've moved forward."

"Elaina, do you know who I am?"

She tilts her head, confused, "Of course, you're Viktor, you own businesses with your brother, including the club I work at."

"Princess, I am the goddamn king of the Solntsvskaya Bratva and it just so happens that scum, Tollfree, owes me a debt. Not only does he owe me money but your innocence. It's time I collect." I step out of the shower quickly and grab her blue towel to dry off with.

Elaina jumps out and swiftly grasps onto my bicep. She uses both hands as one of her hands can only hold onto about half of my bicep.

"Please, Viktor, don't get in trouble. This is my problem, not yours."

"Elaina, an hour ago you became mine, that means your problems became mine. I take care of dirty deeds, it's what I do. I hope you see I'm the one who's truly fucked up." I grab my cell phone out of my pocket to ring Spartak.

"Spartak, you need to stay with Elaina. Call Alexei and Sergei. Tell them to get here and bring the SUV."

"Yes, sir, consider it done."

I hang up and pull my white undershirt on. No point in putting my button up shirt, tie and jacket on. They'd just get dirty with the plans I have.

"Viktor, don't go. He's disrupted my life enough; please don't let him do this to us. Please tell me about the solinska thing."

"The Bratva. You don't know what that is?" I ask, baffled. I thought everyone knew.

"No, I have no idea."

"Are you familiar with Mafia?" She nods her head. "Good, I'm basically the criminal version of the Russkaya Mafiya. It's called the Bratva."

"I see, and you're the leader?"

"Yes, is this an issue?" I retort gruffly.

"It could be. I don't want to live a life hurting people or worrying about you going to jail for the rest of our lives."

"You will hurt no one and you will not know anything about my business, it's not like you think. We can talk about this when I have time. I must go."

"You're making a mistake," she pleads, sadly.

"One thing you will learn, Elaina, is my business is *mine*. Someone has to be willing to make those types of mistakes, just so happens that person is me. You need to accept me for the type of man I am, because I will not change." I kiss her chastely and head out the door.

Chapter 5

Elaina

My mind won't stop reeling. The alcohol has pretty much worn off. I don't think I would've let Viktor go that far if I had been completely sober. I wouldn't change it for anything though. It was time and I'm glad out of everyone, it was him. I feel myself falling a little more for Viktor each time I see him. Now this happens and I know I'm going to be completely infatuated with him. Isn't that what normal girls do with the guy they lose their virginity to?

I can't believe I told him about Brent. I've never admitted that to anyone but with everything happening it just came pouring out. Surprisingly, I feel better now that I've got it out. It seems like any barrier I believed I held, eventually comes crashing down with him. Does it make me a horrible person that I don't feel an ounce of remorse for whatever Viktor's going to do to Brent?

I need to call Emily about this Mafia stuff. Surely she must know about Tate. I grab my phone and quickly close the photo that started this mess of a day. I bet Viktor forgot about it or he'd be looking for two people right now.

***

"Hello? Little sister?"

"Haha, shut it, Emily! You're the younger one."

"Nope. I'm waaay wiser, so that means I win."

"Whatever!"

"So how are you today?"

"Oh my gawd, today was crazy!"

"Why, what happened? Ouch! Baby pains, this kid is a kicker."

"Aww, I love feeling the little one kick. So yeah, crazy day. With Viktor, no less."

She gasps and lets out a little squeal. My sister's been pushing for Viktor and me to get together for months. She's totally on his side and I've been fighting every step of the way. I should have just given in.

"Tell me!"

"Okay, so what's this Mafia business?"

"He told you?!"

"He said it's the Bratva, like Mafia."

"Yeah, not just Bratva, Elaina, he's in charge of all of it. He took over for his uncle. It's kind of a huge thing, you'll learn over time. This life can get crazy but it's also a tight group. Tate and Viktor watch each other's backs and they have a ton of men to protect them."

"So you did know about all of this. Why didn't you say anything about it, ever? I really don't know what to think about it. I don't know if I can handle it like you do."

"I couldn't tell you, I'm sorry but I had to respect Tate's discretion. Of course you can do it. You're as awesome as I am, so you will be fine."

"Ha-ha, thanks. Fairly sure I already know I'm full of awesome though. Anyhow, I love your face, can we eat together soon?"

"Of course, I would love that! I love your face too."

"Bye, Em."

"Bye, little sister."

***

I hang up and sit in the middle of my bed. I'm glad she has faith in me being able to live that life, because I'm not so sure. Me and the Mafia? What kind of things does Viktor even do? I stare at my phone, hoping for it to ring with his number or for his nightly text, only it doesn't come.

Viktor

I'm so angry inside after what she told me, I feel like I have lava coursing through my veins and I can't stop shaking. I had Spartak call my guys because I know I'm too mad to drive. I will probably wreck or kill someone if they cut me off.

My guards show up in the black SUV. I don't think I've ever been so pleased to see them. The windows are so heavily tinted I can't see inside the vehicle. Black is better when transporting bodies, fewer people will see it or pay attention to it at night.

"Stay with her," I bark at Spar and gesture toward Elaina's apartment.

"Yes, sir." He nods and immediately walks toward her door as I quickly jump into the SUV.

Scooting into the middle, I glare at both of my guards. "Alexei! Get Brent Tollfree."

He stares at me in the rearview mirror for a beat, then nods. "You're coming with us, Boss?"

"Of course not, drop me at the warehouse and bring him to me. Make sure he is alive."

"Certainly, sir."

We drive the twenty minutes out of town to one of my warehouses and stop at the one with barely anything inside. It's always deserted unless I pay a visit and it's easier to clean up messes when there isn't much there. The whole place is pretty run down, but it gets the job done for what I use it for.

They drop me off and I give my men their orders to get back as quickly as possible. It's going to feel like ages until they get back. Hopefully Tollfree isn't too messed up, I will thoroughly enjoy being the one inflicting the pain.

Frustrated, I plop down in the single metal chair in the building and drink my vodka straight from the bottle. I'm angry. So fucking mad right now, I don't trust myself to not kill him too quickly if I'm sober. I know the alcohol will slow me down a little and I want to drag this out for a while. I'm going to make him hurt.

I swipe through pictures and stare at the beautiful photos I have of Elaina on my phone. I want her face fresh as I rip this idiot apart. She doesn't know it, but I have many photos of her. Each time she was busy not paying attention and the light would hit her just right I would snap a new one.

I had to have something each night to keep me sane while she was ignoring my advances. Now, she seems to finally realize I'm serious. I wonder if she knows that I'm invested enough I plan to keep her forever? If not, she'll figure it out.

One thing that runs in my family is stubbornness. My father, Tate, and I all have it. If we want something bad enough we will usually make it happen. The only reason my father was stopped, was because Tate and I teamed up to squash him.

Taking in her gorgeous blonde hair, I stroke the photo like a stalker might. I guess in a sense I am a stalker since I follow her around like a fool. The long, pretty locks remind me of that scum at the bar. I wonder if he reminded her of Tollfree and that's why she freaked out.

My rage grows all over again and I impatiently check my watch. Storming angrily over to the square sterile table we use for information extraction, I lay out my preferred tools. I glance over, pleasantly surprised when I'm interrupted by Alexei and Sergei dragging Tollfree in by his ankles.

"He's out?"

"Yes, sir."

"Good, strap him to the table," I order, nodding to the metal brackets and cuffs attached to the table. I enjoy using cuffs so that way if they squirm, it cuts their wrists and ankles. In the end it inflicts even more pain on them.

Alexei and Sergei drag him over and drop him roughly on the table. I walk over and supervise as they clip him in.

"Salts, Sergei."

"Sir." He complies and hands them to me.

I open the small container carefully, placing it under Tollfree's nose. It only takes a second for him to jerk awake, eyes wide, ready to plead.

"Save it." I grab a rag and stuff it in his mouth.

"I want to hear you scream, not your words. Your muffled whimpers will suit me just fine." He shakes his head rapidly at me and tries to plead through the rag.

"I told you when we met that I collect what is owed to me. You hurt someone I love, and that's the biggest debt you can ever owe me."

"Na! Na!" he shouts through the rag.

"No?" I question and he shakes his head. "Ah, but you are mistaken. The answer is yes. You see, I love a sweet little blonde. She reminds me of a fairy, with her long, wispy hair and short legs." He gazes at me, confusion clouding his features.

"I heard you like to touch young girls," I growl and his eyes widen again but this time with a sense of recognition.

"First off, we're going to remove any sense of manhood you may possess, and then I'm going to remove most of your blood. To finish you off... well, I'm going to let you drown. All the way until you sink to the bottom of the lake out back." I nod behind me, toward where the lake is.

By the time I finish with the details, he has tears openly flowing down his face. Good, I hope this trash is terrified. He should be because this is going to hurt, that much I can promise.

I nod to Alexei and he cuts strips in Tollfree's pants so we can easily remove them. "Gloves," I snap and Sergei rushes to get me a pair.

Grasping my tongs tightly, I approach Tollfree's mid-section and his shriveled penis. I snap the tongs together a few good times, causing Tollfree to shriek loudly and attempt to move away.

"Ah!" he cries out, quickly learning that the cuffs will slice into his wrists, and I chuckle for the first time in hours.

I snatch his penis up in my tongs and he goes deathly still. I have to breathe deeply in order to stop myself from squeezing them too forcibly and snap his penis off. I nod to Alexei and he approaches with a small blow torch.

"Hold the tongs; I want to do the burning."

Alexei grabs the tongs in one hand, squeezing Tollfree's penis and making him cry out again. I grin maniacally as I get close to him with the torch. It's going to smell horrible and look disgusting, but my princess deserves to be avenged with every ounce of pain I can cause him.

Carefully aiming the flame at his penis, I watch as the skin burns off it until Alexei drops the tongs. My ears ring with the soul shattering shrieks of a tortured man.

"Shit, Boss, sorry, but they got too hot," Alexei confesses sheepishly.

"It's okay, it was time. He's shit himself, and I want to let him sit in pain for a little while before I continue."

I'm amazed he didn't pass out. Anytime I do penis torture and the meat begins to bubble, the person usually passes out, well, eventually. This is working to my advantage nicely.

I step outside and take a few swigs of my vodka. I need some fresh air. The burnt skin smell is disgusting and makes me nauseous.

"Boss, do you want to tell us what this is about?" Alexei approaches me timidly. He can read my moods pretty well, so he knows I'm in the mood to slaughter someone if they get in my way.

"Not particularly, but I will. He hurt Elaina when she was a little girl." They both look surprised. Sergei then immediately looks angry once he processes what I mean.

"No! That sick fuck!" Alexei, my more emotional guard, whispers, astonished.

I nod in agreement. "Yes. Now do you two understand fully why I must do this?"

They both agree solemnly. Good. I don't care what they say about it anyway. I have already made my mind up.

I head back inside with them both close on my heels. Sending Tollfree an evil smile as he lies there in his own shit, sobbing. I have no sympathy for him, he deserves so much more.

"Now, you have heard of the Bratva bleeding people, yes?" I stare at him as he shakes his head. "No? Okay, well let me enlighten you. It is a signature of Bratva, bloodletting the idiots who cross them. It makes you weak. Only I don't do it the old fashioned way with a little straw. No, I do mine a little differently."

I pull out a large steak knife. I grasp his arm and saw a few large cuts in it, and then I repeat it with each leg and his other arm. When I'm done he has eight large, sawed in cuts on his limbs and his blood trickles out.

"There! Much better," I chortle, throwing my knife in a five gallon bucket full of bleach.

"The dick burning was for my princess, the blood for the Bratva and next, the drowning. That's for my own anger you have caused by making my love doubt her purity."

I sit back in my chair, relaxing, and watch him bleed.

***

I have no concept of time. I just wait until he is weak, but alive enough that he will still suffer when drowning. I nod to my men and they get him up, tying his legs and wrists with brown rope. Alexei hoses the shit off him with the portable pressure washer, that way he doesn't stink up the SUV. Afterwards, they load him up in the back of the vehicle.

We gradually head down to the docks. My men are overly cautious, completely checking out our surroundings on the way. Sergei parks deep in the shadow of one of the buildings.

"Boss?" Alexei questions.

"No, I want to do it alone."

He nods, understanding what this means to me. I climb out using the lit running board step. Alexei opens the hatch, illuminating the back trunk area.

I pull all of the concrete weights out. Their heaviness forces me to take my time. I place the weights and rope down on the dock for later.

Rushing, I return excitedly for the body. This will probably end up being the kill I appreciate the most out of any other. Hauling him over my shoulder, fireman style, I carry him closer to the water.

Warm, syrupy liquid coats my fingers, bleeding onto my hands and drips to the cold cement below. The sky is black, the stars and moon hiding, helping me complete my task. The calming *swoosh* of the waves mask my noises as I drop the lifeless body to the ground to finish securing weights to his limbs.

He's almost dead, but not quite. I can't help the elation I feel in the pit of my stomach. I've gotten used to this part over time and it's now become my absolute favorite.

The small pier is deserted and the men on the docks know to mind their own business. There aren't many around here at this time of night. No one wants to be involved with the Bratva, especially when its leader is dumping bodies. They keep their concerns to themselves, knowing they would be next on my list.

I relish the feeling of such power. I never said I was a good man, I said I clean up messes. I'm the dark angel, waiting to take care of the dirty deeds of the Mafiya.

I was the smart one, the one strictly handling the money of the business. I didn't want anything to do with this life, and then my uncle gave me my first taste of disposal. I don't necessarily enjoy the kill itself, but I love watching them sink into the deep, murky waters of the lakes surrounding us. This kill though – this one I will enjoy every single moment of.

He stares at me in a daze and I can't help but smile.

"You asked for this when you touched that innocent little girl. She couldn't defend herself, so now I come for you, and here you are, helpless. I hope you experience this feeling up until the moment death comes to collect you." I end my speech by spitting on the trash.

I stand up and kick him, rolling the weights along until he eventually tumbles into the deep, dark water. I want every last minute leading up to his death to be miserable.

Chapter 6

Elaina
Three days later...

I can't believe it, I still haven't heard from him. I fucking knew he wouldn't want me once he found out about me and my baggage. It's just like Stephanie all over again, except this hurts worse. I've been sitting in my apartment moping and waiting for him for three days. It's time I got up and looked for a new job.

I grab my purse and make my way outside. Spartak is in his car, reading a book. I walk over and peer in at the book. *Pride and Prejudice.* Hmmm, I never would have guessed. When I knock on his window lightly he jumps, startled, and turns to me. Cocking his eyebrow, he rolls down the window and grins.

"Time for work?"

"No, what are you doing out here?"

He looks at me, puzzled. "The same as always." He shrugs "Reading new books."

"Viktor didn't call you off?"

"No. Mr. Viktor would kill me if I left."

"How long have you been here?"

"For three days."

"Three days?!" I gasp, astonished. "Where have you gone to the bathroom, and what about eating?"

"I used the bushes and I have food in the trunk."

"You haven't left at all?"

"Nope."

"Holy shit! Come on."

"Where?"

"You're taking a shower at my place."

"No, thank you. The boss would get upset and a shower is not worth risking my life over."

"What on earth could he get angry about?"

"About me being inside your apartment."

"Oh! Gotcha! Okay, well then you stay alive and stinky and I will drive around looking for a new job." I smile and shrug.

"What's wrong with your old job?"

"I walked out in the middle of it the other day."

"Doesn't matter, Tate owns it and Viktor runs it for him. You could go in there and sit on the bar stool and you'd still get paid."

I look at him, stunned. "Are you serious?"

"Yes, ma'am, I'm serious."

"Well, then I'm going to work and I'm wearing my shorts," I respond tartly. He beams a smile and nods.

So Viktor hasn't called me, but he keeps his guy on me and I still have my job. I really don't understand him at all and I ponder this as I head toward my car.

I arrive to work and everyone acts normal, like I just had a day off or something. It feels like I'm walking around in the Twilight Zone. Maybe I really could do whatever I want and not get in trouble. Nice.

I clock in and start my regular set up. Might as well; I have nothing else to do, but worry about *him* and I will lose my head if I sit and dwell on it all day. I feel sort of guilty. I bet Hawk was dragged over here to cover the shifts I've missed. I'll have to apologize the next time I see him.

An hour or so goes by and I hear keys clink on the bar. Turning, I'm faced with Viktor sitting in his normal spot, grinning at me as if he hasn't been absent from my life for half the week. I don't know whether to be excited or angry right now.

"Can I have my usual?" he murmurs and my pussy clenches when I hear his voice. I swallow and nod.

I go through the motions of making his vodka-seven with lime wedge. I place it before him on top of a bar napkin and he smiles sweetly at me. Bastard has some nerve popping up like everything's just dandy.

"Ugh." I huff, irritated, and turn to finish my shift duties. The more I do now, the less I'll have to worry about later.

"You are displeased with me?"

Rolling my eyes, I sigh and look at his gorgeous face. "I'm upset that once you found out about me you left." I shrug as I reply bluntly.

He looks taken aback for a moment before he adopts a serious expression. "I didn't leave you. I told you I was taking care of the problem. I would never just leave you without a purpose. I had a big issue needing to be handled, so I took care of it."

"You took care of it? How exactly do you take care of something like that?" I ask, exasperated.

"You will never be faced with him again for the rest of your life," Viktor says proudly.

"Well, that's a relief I suppose, but I hadn't seen him in a long time anyhow. I told you I just want to forget that stuff."

"Well, now it's forever. You won't ever see him again." Just the way he says it makes me suspect something entirely different than what I had originally imagined, like him moving away or something.

"Tell me what you did." I am beginning to get scared for Viktor's safety and freedom.

"My business, Elaina, is not yours about that kind of stuff. It's my job to protect you and know that I am protecting you as much as I can." I nod and bite my lip.

"So you didn't leave me then, you're still around for me?"

"I'm right here, watching you, wanting you, as I have since I first laid eyes on you." He states all this in a raspy voice as he runs his eyes all over my body, pausing on my breasts and hips.

"Okay, good."

"Good, as in I can stop chasing you?"

I shrug. "Maybe, but only if you like me."

He laughs loudly. "Ah, Princess! Of course I like you." I give him a large smile, recalling our conversation in his car when he kissed me.

"I kind of like you, too."

"Oh, so finally you concede, and admit it." He chuckles and I smile back at him.

"Hey, bar wench!" We're interrupted by a whiny voice. I swear I shoot daggers as I face Kendall.

"Yes, whore?" I retort in a nice, chipper voice. I want to test this theory that I can do what I want and Viktor will let me keep my job.

"Whore?" she screeches and I wince. "You have some nerve! Viktor, you see how this trash speaks to me?"

He rolls his eyes, grunts, and looks over at me. I shrug.

"Look, Mob Candy, get your painted ass out of here." I sneer back at her.

"Ugh! Viktor, Daddy will hear about this!"

He stands and faces her. "Kendall, get out of my club. You just insulted my bar manager who happens to also be my princess. You can leave or I will have my men remove you."

Viktor nods at Sergei who comes to intercept her and get her to leave. She pouts at Sergei, but he still escorts her to the door. Viktor turns back to me and I could maul him right now. I can't believe he stuck up for me and said that stuff to her.

"You're pretty awesome," I state and smirk at him.

"Oh, you think so?" He smirks back, showing off his sexy dimple.

"So I'm your manager and princess, huh?"

"If you want the position, it's yours."

"To be your princess?"

"Yes, and the club manager, since you won't let me fully take care of you."

"You're serious?"

"I am completely serious. Now, what will your answer be?"

"Of course it's yes!" I yell, leaning over the counter and planting a kiss on his lips.

He freezes, surprised, then pulls me over further on the counter and takes my mouth in a toe-curling kiss.

Viktor

"But what about Todd?" she asks after kissing me soundly and completely surprising me.

"Don't worry about him, if you want the job then I can send him to my father's club with Hans."

Hell, I will even buy Elaina a club if she would like one. I know she would never go for it, but I really would. I want to make her life easier any way I can.

"Yaay! Okay, thank you so much!" she says excitedly and jumps up and down a few times. I chuckle at her enthusiasm. She works very hard and deserves it.

"Now, can we go to dinner since you are the boss here?"

"I think we can celebrate!"

Elaina lets the other bartender know she's leaving, grabs her things and meets me at my stool.

"Mind if I?"

I gesture with my hand and wrap my arm around her waist to pull her close as I stand up. She freezes up for a moment, her body going still like a statue. I grasp her face and turn it up to mine, gazing tenderly in her eyes. I wish she could see it in the way I look at her. She needs to realize I would never hurt her or touch her in any unwanted way.

Elaina studies me for a minute and I feel her muscles start to relax. She smiles and kisses me softly. To see her so happy makes my heart feel so full, as if it could burst. I hold her closely and nod to Alexei so he knows we are leaving.

We make our way out the back door to my car. Elaina lets loose a blood-curdling scream, making chills crawl up my spine. She covers her face with her hands, ducking behind me.

I scan the area but notice nothing amiss at first. I look to the driver's seat because Sergei should have the door open for us, only I don't see him. I diligently look over everything again.

Elaina whimpers softly behind me and I reach back, squeezing her hand, attempting to comfort her. The bright light glints off the Mercedes and for the first time I notice the front of the vehicle. Sergei is laid out on the hood, throat slit, covered in dark blood.

I walk toward him, noticing something on the windshield. The club door bangs as it slams closed. I jump a little, ready to protect Elaina with my life if necessary. Twisting, I find Alexei, looking at me, perplexed.

"Shit! Boss?" He moves to do an area search.

"No. Stay with Elaina." I growl at him and remove my gun, screwing on my silencer. I'm going to kill any of them that I find still here. They have nerve, coming at *me*, the king of the Bratva. I will feed each one to the fish if necessary. Whoever did this deserves to hurt. They will pay; I will make sure of it.

I carefully walk around the car and scan the surroundings but I find no one. I return to the front of the vehicle, and move closer to check on Sergei. He is very much dead and across the windshield in his blood, is smeared WAR.

It's sloppy, so I know they were in a hurry to get out of here, as they should have been. This club is crawling with my men. I can't believe there wasn't any other guards back here with him.

Just when things start to look up with Elaina, I am faced with this. I can't let her get hurt in any of this nonsense. I pull my phone out and call Spartak.

"Sir?"

"Spar, bring the car around back quickly!"

"Yes, sir!"

I hang up, watching our surroundings the best I can. I make my way back to Elaina. I keep her behind me against the club wall just in case someone comes at us, I can protect her better this way.

"Poor, poor Sergei!" She sniffles, grasping onto the back of my suit jacket with one hand.

"I know. We need to call his family. I will make sure they are taken care of, it's the least I can do."

"He has a family?" she enquires gloomily. "God! This is all my fault." She starts to sob.

"No, lovely, this is some demented little girl stirring the pot to something she has no idea about. You did nothing wrong and I can assure you, this will be handled."

I can't believe this is happening. I have to call Tate and get everything prepared just in case this really is war. If so, none of us are safe.

"Alexei, put Sergei in the trunk for now and transport him to the warehouse until we can arrange a proper burial for him. Get the car cleaned up and trade it in for a new one." I'm not a big enough bastard to make him continue to drive the same car around. It's bad enough he's stuck cleaning it up.

"Okay, Boss." He glowers at the car, furious, upset that his workmate was murdered.

"I apologize, I know he was your friend."

"He was a good man, Boss."

"I know. You both are," I answer solemnly as Spartak arrives with the other car.

Elaina and I climb in, hastily shutting the door and Spartak drives off immediately.

"Duck down, Elaina." I push her head down as we exit the alleyway.

You can never be too careful. I want her safe and I wouldn't be surprised if someone is waiting for us to leave. Spar shoots me a wary look in the rearview mirror.

"Spartak, take us to my house, then go back with one of the guys to sweep Elaina's car. Use caution, I wouldn't doubt it if they did something to it."

Elaina gasps and turns to me, surprised, "My car! I can't lose my vehicle, Viktor!"

"You won't lose it, Elaina, that's why Spartak will check on it. He can even drive it elsewhere if you would like." Nodding somberly, she leans on me, worried.

I tap his shoulder lightly, murmuring quietly, "Pick her car up and park it in my garage."

"No problem, sir." Agreeing, he faces forward and I clutch Elaina tightly to my chest.

What on earth am I getting this beautiful creature into? I promise I will do everything in my power to make sure she doesn't witness that sort of thing again. She has had enough negativity in her life. I don't need to add to it.

The car ride is eerily silent. It feels like we drive for forever. I busy myself by concentrating on what needs to be done. I'm sure Elaina's playing that scene repeatedly in her head while Spartak gives his full attention to our surroundings. He's on high alert because you never know who or what could be coming next when you're in a war.

Chapter 7

Viktor

I open the garage with my cell phone app and we pull in. After the club incident, I can't help but glance all around, scanning everything for a potential threat. I want every corner and bush checked; I'm paranoid and it makes me even more irritated. I've gone through a mini war before with my uncle, years back. Many people died pretty gruesome deaths.

Leaning closer to Spartak I say sternly, "I will rearm the system. You take the guard room." I can't help my tone, I'm tense and angry. I need to release this pent up energy before I shoot someone.

"Thank you, sir," he replies, unfazed, and heads inside first to do a sweep.

My home is very secure but we take every precaution when something like this pops off. You can never be too careful. I'm fortunate to have good men on my side, even if I am hard to work for sometimes.

I mumble quietly, "Come, lovely," and grasp Elaina's hand.

Swiftly, I lead her down the plain hallway toward my office. There are no pictures or little decorations, just light grey walls and dark hardwood floors. It's simple and tidy, just the way I prefer.

Undoing my shirt buttons and cuff links the best I can with one hand, I prepare. There's only one thing I can think of right now to get me to calm down, and that's Elaina. The only decision I want to have to make right now is whether to feast on her cunt or spank it.

"Your office?" she inquires curiously and I smirk.

"Yes, Princess." I growl, focused and eager, removing my jacket and shirt.

Her eyes widen and she takes a step backward. "But I—"

Interrupting her, I reach out and bring her close to me, taking her mouth with mine. Her hands land on my chest and I pull her tight against my body. I know she has to feel my hard cock resting against her tummy. Now's not the time to move sluggishly. I needed her twenty minutes ago, and I need her even more so now.

I walk backwards, pulling her along. Eventually I bump into my desk and stop, perching on the edge. Releasing her mouth, I loosen my belt buckle and unbutton my pants.

Elaina leans back, lips red and glistening, her eyes lit up with fire. "What do you want, Viktor?" she asks me boldly and my cock strains against my boxers.

Leaning up slightly, I push them off my hips so they pool at my feet. She licks her lips and I weave my hands through her smooth, Cinderella-like locks. I push her down easily until she rests on her knees, staring up at me with her bright blue, curious irises.

I grin at her as if she's my prey. "Kiss it," I purr and she gulps, staring at my dick, intimidated.

Releasing her hair, I tip her chin up and press my thumb between her soft lips. She sucks automatically so I pull her chin closer. She leisurely releases my finger, coated in her sugary lip gloss. I bring it to my own mouth, copying her and sucking the sweetness off.

Elaina gasps slightly, nose flaring and leans in, taking my throbbing member into her mouth. "Yes, like that," I mutter huskily, pleased.

I curl my toes inside my shoes, attempting to stop the craving to grab her hair roughly and thrust until she chokes on my cock. I can just imagine her shocked expression and the tears that would float down her cheeks afterwards. *Mm.*

I know I have to be vigilant with her needs and not give her too much time to think. If she thinks, bad memories will creep in, and I want to steal every negative thought away from her. I snatch her up swiftly by her chin. She squeaks as she stands, surprise clouding her features.

I huff, "It was perfect, love," and turn her hastily so she's now perched on the desk, with me standing instead.

Her skirt hikes up, offering the perfect little glimpse of her white panties. Taking two fingers I slide them over.

"Viktor!" She gasps against my mouth when I check how wet she is.

Rubbing softly in circles, I prime her pussy, coating it in wetness. Her body trembles with need each time I apply pressure to her clit. Gazing into her eyes, I stop, pulling my hand back slightly to spank her plump little pussy lips three times.

"Oh!" Elaina mewls, crinkling her eyes in pleasurable pain, and I grin.

I dip my finger in her nectar, covering her clit in it. Once it's nice and saturated, I pull my hand back, spanking her pussy two more times, then grind my palm back and forth into her clit, relentlessly at the end. She leans forward suddenly, resting her head on my chest as she cries out. Her cunt soaks my fingers in her cum.

I draw back, thoroughly turned on, pumping my dick with her juices a few times. Her cheeks flush as she stares at me hungrily.

Gripping her hip in one hand, I line myself up and shove my cock forcefully in her tight pussy.

"Oh shit!" Elaina moans loudly, spurring me on and I thrust in deeper.

"Just lean back, love, and let me take that cunt like I want to."

She relaxes her body, lying down and I shove her shirt up so her breasts are free. I don't want sweet right now, I want to fuck. Hard.

Placing my large hand in the middle of Elaina's chest, I hold her down securely on the hefty cherry desk. Her breasts sway with each hard pump. Her nipples are stiff and begging for my touch.

"Oh my!" she mewls loudly.

I'm sure Spartak can hear each little noise from her, but I don't mind. Pulling her fingers back to my mouth, I suck strongly on each digit making her pussy pulse snugly over and over. Each time she clenches, my cock screams with want.

I pound into her savagely, moving my hips in an up and down motion, trying to reach her perfect place, her sweet spot. With each up motion I shake the desk and make the wood creak. Her mouth gapes as she watches me suck and release each of her fingers.

Snarling, I attempt to hold myself back. She just feels too good and I want her so badly. Her body sings when I touch it. It's like her skin is waiting to be pressed against mine and when it finally happens we both ignite.

"If your pussy doesn't behave, I'm going to end up finishing a lot quicker than I want to," I tell her. As soon as the words leave my lips she calls out my name, her chest heaving as she regains the breath stolen by the strong orgasm.

Thoroughly spent, she stares at me in a daze as I grip her breast and spill myself deep inside her.

"Perfection," I utter, replete.

Elaina blinks as if coming out of a daze and moves to get up.

"Stay." I shove her back down and she huffs as she shoots me an irritated look. She doesn't like it when I boss her around.

I gently pull myself out of her, shivering at the aftershock zing of sensations. I grin and quickly make my way to the bathroom that's connected to my office and get a warm, wet wash cloth. It's my cum dripping out of her, so the least I can do is clean it up for her.

"What are you doing, Viktor?"

"I'm cleaning you. Would you prefer to take a bath?"

"No, thank you, but I can do that."

"Nonsense, Princess," I grumble and start wiping her skin softly with the white fluffy towel.

She scrambles away slightly "No, please stop." She covers her breasts.

"What's going on? I was absent not even two minutes. What changed between then and now?" I gesture to the bathroom, confused.

"I just like a little privacy. I would like to do that on my own. You're watching me and cleaning me."

"Yes, I want to take care of you. Why is this a problem? Of course I'm watching you, you're stunning."

"Please. The watching and touching," Elaina replies softly, bowing her head.

I let loose a growl, getting exceptionally angry. "The touching!" I yell, "Fuck!" Throwing the towel down beside her I storm a few steps away. "That *thing* will never touch you again! You want to know why?" I step closer, clenching my fists. I feel as if I could rip apart my office right now. "You know why? I'll tell you why! Because I watched that pathetic *thing*, sink to the bottom of the lake after I burned his tiny penis off with a fucking blow torch! So don't you cringe from me! I am NOTHING like him! I have waited, *months* for you! Months! I will never harm you." I rip my hands through my hair, pulling harshly, and I cringe, angry, defeated.

I rush back to the bathroom for a large towel, thrust it at her and turn away. Not because I am upset with her, but because I am so irate at the thought of someone causing her any type of harm. I will make it my life's mission to keep her safe. To an extent I already have been protecting her. But now, *now* she is mine. I have had every piece of her and I don't intend to ever give that up to anyone else. If I need to have five men on her at all times to make sure nothing ever happens to her, I will. I will flatten whoever crosses her in life if I need to.

She will learn that she is stronger now. She not only has me beside her, but behind her as well. I will always come for her when needed and she needs to realize that no one will ever hurt her as long as I have breath.

Hearing sniffling, I turn to quickly glance at her. She has a tear tumbling down her cheek and it makes my gut clench. "Lovely, please talk to me, please tell me what I can do to fix it?" I say softly, gently.

She looks at me with heartbreak in her eyes, "That's just it, Viktor. You can't fix it. I'll always be broken."

"No, Elaina, you are strong, you know why?"

She bites her bottom lip and shakes her head.

"You, my love, are strong, because not only did you survive, but you escaped. Instead of staying and succumbing to that life, you worked and left as soon as possible. You, Princess, you are an inspiration. I am proud to have you." I say this genuinely, staring at her in awe, full of love and respect. *How can she not know how wonderful she is?*

She sits silent, processing everything I said and I leave to my bedroom. She really does need some privacy to pull herself together. I know she will, she's stubborn and that stubbornness has kept her strong over the years.

***

I'm standing in the middle of my bedroom in my boxer briefs after my shower when Spartak calls me through the intercom system.

"Mr. Masterson?"

"It's okay, Spartak, I'm alone."

"Right, well, boss, we had an issue come up."

"Go on."

"We found a note and some pictures of you with Kendall at lunch on Miss Elaina's car and a mini starter bomb was wired."

"Spartak, what did I tell you about calling her by her first name?"

"I apologize, sir, but she told me to go by first names."

"If that's what she wants then. Everyone was okay handling her car?"

"Yes, we just loaded it on a trailer to take it to the old warehouse out of the way."

"Good idea. Hold on to the note and pictures, I want to see if they are like the one Elaina had on her phone."

"Yes, Boss. Sir, umm I think you two should head to the cabin. This is looking like it could turn serious."

"I'll get Elaina. Tell the housekeeper to pack what we need."

"Of course, sir."

***

Elaina

I step out of Viktor's enormous office shower and grab a fluffy white towel. People often don't put much thought into towels, but geez what a difference it makes. My towels at home feel like rough carpet compared to these.

I'm so grateful he gave me some privacy and a little time to cool down. Twenty minutes can have a huge impact when you're on the verge of a meltdown. I was awash with too many emotions all at once, I felt as if I was drowning trying to express how I was feeling.

I'm interrupted mid-drying and mid-thought, by an agitated Viktor. Christ, this man needs to drink a vodka-seven and take a breather.

"Yes? I wasn't drying off or anything."

Viktor hears my sarcasm and raises an eyebrow, slowly scanning my body. He starts at the foot propped up on the side of the tub. He follows my calf to my thigh, pausing for a beat. He gazes between my thighs taking in a deep breath as he catalogs my pussy.

I watch, amused, as he licks his lips while looking at my breasts until he makes his way to my eyes. I shoot him a peeved look, raising my eyebrows and flaring my nostrils, all though I'm fairly entertained after that long glance he just gave me.

Vik grunts and says sternly, "Stop fooling around, Elaina. I'm here because we need to head to another one of my places."

Snorting, I playfully reply, "Really? I was under the impression you were in here to stare at me. Surely you can't be hungry for more already?"

He studies my eyes for a moment as he grits his teeth, then he practically growls, "You have no clue what my appetite can be like." Viktor quickly scans my body again, "Get dressed and get to the Jag." With that he turns, slamming the bathroom door behind him.

That went well. He's normally so sweet to me and helpful all the time; this moody shit has my head spinning. I know he's stressed out about everything going on, but this sucks. I feel like he wants to put me over his knee and spank me for being bad or something.

I pull my skirt and shirt on from before since I don't have the luxury of a change of clothes here. I refuse to wear dirty underwear though, and Viktor got them soaked earlier. *Hmm, where can I put these?* I snatch a fluffy washcloth to roll them up in and toss them into my ginormous purse.

I venture out of his office in search of the garage door from earlier. I know we pretty much just walked straight but his house is huge; like fit-ten-of-my-apartment–inside-his-house type huge. I should have asked him if he turned that alarm thing off. *Ugh! Where is that man?*

I glance into a sitting area as I walk down the hall, another bathroom and what looks to be the entry to the kitchen, but no Viktor. Stubborn man will just have to get over his temper tantrum if I trip the alarm. At least I'll know where he is if I do.

After the lengthy hallway I end up at the giant metal door we came in from. I make it through and thankfully there are no lights or sirens and no metal blinds coming down over everything. I release my pent up breath that I hadn't realized I had been holding since I walked in the door, and head toward Viktor's beautiful Jaguar.

I lightly graze my fingertips along the smooth lines. I wonder if he would let me drive this bad boy. I know she's a whole lot faster than my little white Camaro. I love my car but come on, this is a Jaguar! Surely he won't have it unlocked, being Mr. Security. Screw it, if the alarm goes off, oh well. I seem to be a little risk taker today anyhow.

I lightly pull the door handle and sure enough it comes open silently and smoothly. I slide right in. I'm already this far, so I'm going to sit here and soak up the brilliant feel of the leather and imagine myself making this beauty jet down the highway.

I feel something cold press against my temple and my lungs seize up immediately. *Oh my gawd.*

"Click-Clack, *bitch*. Guess who's going to be bleeding now?"

No. Fucking. Way. I know that voice. I don't know if I can speak though as my stomach churns crazily. Bile starts to climb my esophagus and I clench my throat closed tightly. I'm fairly sure I just want to puke all over everything. I've never had a gun held to my head and I'm not sure what the fuck to do. This bitch is just plain stupid.

"Kendall, are you crazy? This is Viktor's house! When he finds you, he will slaughter you!" I wheeze, breathing deeply to try to keep from expelling my stomach contents all over Viktor's butter-smooth interior. "How on earth did you even get in here?"

Kendall laughs shrilly and I clench my eyes closed at the noise. "You dumb piece of filth. You really think I would come alone? I'm not stupid. You thought you could humiliate me in that club? I don't think so, bitch. Viktor is supposed to be mine. He doesn't need to be wasting time on you!"

"If Viktor sees you in here doing this then any chance you think you may have had of having him, will be gone. Think about this for a minute."

Kendall shoves the gun against my temple harshly and I wince.

"Shut up!" she screeches in her nasally voice.

There's a loud crash to the side of us. Kendall turns to watch Alexei tackle her man and I use the distraction to try to get the gun away. I will probably end up being shot regardless, but it's better than point blank range in the side of the head.

I grip onto her wrists tightly, growling and thrusting her arms away from me. Kendall fights back, desperately trying to aim the gun at me. I struggle, screaming at her angrily, fighting for my life.

She shrilly yells, "Let go, you cunt!"

"No way, you psycho! Give it to me!" I scream, leaning over to bite a chunk out of her boney little arm. I move her arms back and forth as much as I can, attempting to free the weapon from her.

Suddenly I'm hit with a blinding pain on the side of my head; it momentarily dazes me and I lose focus of what I'm doing. I release my teeth and let go of her arms, trying to blink and shake away the pain. *Ouch.*

I feel like I've been hit with a Mack truck, and I realize I'd let go of the gun. Turning rapidly I see the gun pointed at me for a split second. I gasp in a deep breath and close my eyes. This is it, I'm dead. I wait for a beat then hear Kendall scream savagely.

I open my eyes and see the back door open, with Viktor bent inside the car. Viktor has Kendall in a tight choke hold with one arm and has his other arm pointing her hand with the gun toward the ceiling.

I swear it's like a rush of adrenaline hits me as I leap through the two front seats. I grab her tit in one hand and squeeze as hard as I can. She starts stomping her feet and I get kneed in the face as I lean over to take a large bite of her exposed thigh.

Kendall wails and lets go of the gun, flailing her arms crazily. My hair is ripped upward for a second before she is dragged out of the vehicle. Alexei is there waiting and grabs Kendall forcefully from behind.

She glares spitefully at me. "You stupid bitch! I will kill you, I promise you that. And if I don't, then my daddy will kill all of you!" Alexei yanks her arms back even further and I swear they could pop out at any time. He mutters something in her ear and she shakes her head angrily.

Suddenly a hand pops in front of me. Blinking rapidly, following it, I meet Viktor's worried gaze. I grab it tightly and let him pull me out of his beautiful, mistreated car.

"Princess?" he inquires quietly.

I shake my head. "No, you got here in time. I'm alright."

"You're sure?"

"Yes, I'm okay." I nod and attempt to fix my screwed up clothes. It looks like I just took a roll through some prickly bushes. I can only imagine what my hair looks like after that spaz got ahold of it.

Viktor takes a step back and in doing so, reveals the man Kendall had brought with her. Only now, the guy is on the floor. He's perched on his knees, badly beaten and in handcuffs.

"You realize, Kendall, that I get retribution now, right? I know you have heard the stories, probably from your own father about me. Is that why you've become so infatuated with me?"

She adopts her naïve, innocent expression and attempts to appear coy with him. "Retribution for what, Viktor? Daddy said we were meant for each other, so I was only taking care of this pest for you."

Viktor's eyes widen. "Meant for each other? That's positively ludicrous. You don't have a chance; you're not even on my radar, Kendall." He turns toward her man and raises Kendall's gun— "You took a very close guard from me"—and shoots her guard right center in his forehead.

The guard drops to the ground and I swallow forcefully. Kendall starts laughing like a hyena and looks at me happily. She really is insane.

She nods to me, grinning. "Look at her, Viktor! She can't even handle a kill! I'm not worried about it, he was just a guard. I will easily get another."

Viktor glares at her as if he wants to kill her. "Consider this is your only warning. Tell your father that next time I will not hesitate to kill you." Viktor nods to Alexei and he starts to drag her toward the door, she giggles as he does and it shoots chills down my body.

That chick is a complete Looney Tunes. I'm now sure that she wouldn't have hesitated to shoot me. She gave off that impression when we were fighting in the car, but one can always hope that the other person is not as bad as they appear. I don't know how Viktor does it. He looked completely blank when he pulled that trigger. I know he said he ran the Bratva, but it feels like that title is really hitting me full force right now. I like to think he would never hurt me like that, but he looked completely zoned out. It didn't affect him at all to pull that trigger. I may be on the tougher side, but I could never kill anyone like that. What on earth have I gotten myself into?

I notice the guard's blood and cough, rushing to the side of the vehicle. I regurgitate everything left in my stomach all over Viktor's shiny grey, speckled garage floor. After blowing chunks for a few minutes I feel a hand on my back.

I can't help but cringe away. I can't be touched right now, especially by a hand that brought someone pain. The guy was bad, here to hurt me, but it still screws with my head.

Viktor murmurs and it brings tears to my eyes. "My love, please."

I have no clue what it means, but the Russian sounds so beautiful, it flows out of his mouth like water flows down a stream. Hiccupping, I take in his features. Even after committing murder, he's beautiful. His hazel eyes stare longingly at me, worried and sad. Why? I have no idea, but I'm curious.

"What, Viktor?" I tremble and the first tear makes its way down my flushed cheeks.

He reaches his hand toward me slowly, cautiously, gazing at me fearfully. "Please, don't fear me, Elaina," he replies softly.

Nodding, I reach out and accept his hand. I know I should be more cautious, but he promised long ago to never hurt me. Viktor promised my sister and Tate, I know this, Emily told me. I have to trust that, right? My gut tells me he will protect me and to go to him. My gut usually tells the truth, I'm not sure yet about my heart, and lord knows my mind is torn on what to do.

He pulls me toward him. I hop over the puke and let him clutch me tightly to his chest. He whispers something into my hair but I can't hear him over my sobs. It's surreal, like I have no idea I'm even crying this hard. I didn't pull the trigger, so why is it affecting me so strongly?

"Shh, shh, it's okay, Princess. Calm down, it's over with now," he says as he delicately pets my hair. It's soothing and after a few moments, I'm able to slow the flow of tears and catch my breath. I hate being a mess and not being able to pull myself together right away. I'm usually pretty decent at hiding my emotions. I guess murder is my breaking point. God. Murder.

We're all going to go to jail now. Fuck. I can't believe this, I wonder if the cops are on their way right now. Did anyone hear that gun shot? The neighbors aren't that close, but still the garage had to have echoed. Damn, I wish I could hear if there are sirens coming. What can I do? Run? Yeah right.

No, this is Viktor, he said he cleans stuff up and takes care of things. The way he looked, surely he knows what to do. He'll know how to clean this up and, knowing his stubbornness, he will take care of everything. I need to chill out and see if he will tell me his plan.

"What's going to happen?" I ask foggily, gazing past him to the ceiling. I can't focus on him right now, I'm scared what I may find in his eyes if I look at them right now.

"Lovely, this is Bratva business. I will fix it and keep you safe." I blink, cataloging his scruffy jaw while he speaks then stare off solemnly for a few moments. Right, this is his business.

"I just don't know what to think right now," I utter and he nods understandingly at me.

"I know, and we will discuss it more later. For now we need to get into the car. Alexei and Spartak are coming with us. My house has obviously been compromised. I had the alarm off for ten minutes and that loophole was utilized by my enemies. I will not take any more chances with your safety. I would never forgive myself if anything were to happen to you," he says kindly and helps me back into his Jaguar.

The guys load up and next thing I know we are driving along through hills full of trees. I have no clue how long we drive, but it feels like I stare out of the window for hours.

Chapter 8

I must have fallen asleep during the ride because I awake drowsy and confused. I take in my strange surroundings. We're parked in front of a beautiful little log cabin, and it appears to be surrounded by forest.

There's a small private gravel drive that ends in front of the charming little porch. It has four steps leading up to the door and a hanging bench swing off to the side. I bet it would be amazing to sit out here on the swing in the morning, sipping a sweet coffee or hot chocolate.

It feels like we are enclosed into our own little bubble. The trees and bushes make a natural curtain around us. There's a detached garage or shop building off to the side, and a little toward the back of the cabin, all along the side is lined with rows upon rows of chopped wood.

"Miss Elaina?" I'm brought out of my thoughts by Spartak.

"Yes, Spartak? Where are we?"

"Come inside please, ma'am. The boss had me wait out here until you awoke, but wants you inside as soon as possible."

"He made you wait for me? That's crazy! Where are we exactly?"

"We are at Mr. Masterson's cabin."

"You don't say? Clearly I can see we're at his cabin! I meant as in *here* here. Where are we? Are we even in Tennessee still?" I ask dramatically and he blushes a little.

"Oh. Yes. We are just in the mountains, didn't leave the state or anything. You actually weren't asleep for that long."

"Hmm, it feels like it. I thought we drove for forever." I slide across the leather seat and make my way out of the car.

Poor guy has been stuck on babysitting duty for me again. Ugh, my neck is stiff and my jaw is sore. It must be from Kendall. I have no idea what to do about her and I don't want to even think about it right now. I need to find Viktor and figure out what he plans on us doing.

I glance over at Spartak as I make my way to the porch stairs. "Say, Spartak?"

"Yes, ma'am?" He looks over at me curiously and follows me up the stairs.

"Where is Viktor anyhow?"

"He's inside handling business."

I step to the side for Spartak to enter first. "What is his business, anyhow?"

"He has a storage business."

"Sure, if that's what you call it."

He smirks a little at me then shakes his head, locking the thick wood door securely behind me.

The inside of the cabin is just as fairytalesque as the outside. I wouldn't have believed in a thousand years this was Viktor's had I not driven here with him. His house seemed very plain and sterile; whereas here it's quaint and homey feeling.

There's a giant fireplace as the focal point with a large square rug in front of it. The tan couches look more worn than new, but the kind of worn where you know they are really comfortable. A few wooden side tables with lamps and coasters resting on them are placed conveniently around the couches. There are family photos all along the decorative mantle, many of Viktor and Tate. They seem to be so different, yet so alike at the same time.

The living area is open and leads into a cozy kitchen. The kitchen is decorated in a wine theme, with matching pictures and hand towels to coordinate. I can't make out much more besides a wooden staircase and a hallway. I'm guessing the bedrooms are upstairs.

"Does he come here a lot?" I gesture around the living room, taking in all the small details.

"When he gets some time off he does, especially in the summer. This is Mishka's favorite place."

"Oh! That's his gran, right? I think that's the name Emily had told me was hers."

"Yep, she comes sometimes and will cook for us, good Russian meals. I haven't eaten like that since I was last in Russia with my family."

"Wow, Russia! When were you in Russia last?" I hear Viktor on the phone as he comes closer to the living room, he tells whomever he's speaking to that they need to hold on for just a second.

"Elaina, that's enough. Spartak, go do a perimeter check," Viktor barks and I scowl at him in return.

"We were having a conversation," I bite back and Spar looks like a deer trapped in headlights. I see his Adam's apple bob quickly as he gulps and rushes toward the door. I don't know what that was all about but whatever. He may boss Spartak around all the time, but he's lost his marbles if he thinks I'm okay with him talking to me that way.

"Yes, I will get back to you," Viktor says in a monotone voice to the caller and hits end, pocketing the cell phone.

He looks at me, amused, then steps closer, adopting the look of a hunter stalking his prey. He circles around me and I stand stock still, waiting for the yelling or anger to come. Whatever I did, Spartak sure was quick to bolt. Thanks, friend. If it ever comes down to it, I guess I know who my allies are.

I feel warm breath close to my ear, caressing my skin, giving me goose bumps, and my stomach flip flops crazily. I draw in a deep silent gasp of air, holding it, trying to be as still as possible. I don't have a clue why I'm still trying to not move, but it just seems like the right thing to do. Like when you're faced with a powerful beast and you're told to stand still so as to not provoke it. This man makes my body go wild for him, stirring up emotions and feelings I've never encountered before.

In a raspy rumble close to my ear he says, "You don't need to be nosing in his business. You are here for me, not him." He licks up the outer shell of my ear and I squeak slightly, licking my lips in return. It's like a conditioned response, picturing him licking me in *other* places.

"Now, be a good girl and go wash up for dinner. Bathroom's through there." He brushes along my arm to point and I shudder in response to his nearness.

I nod silently and rush to the restroom. Holy shit, that man completely throws me off balance. I can't even remember what I was saying to him before he licked my ear. Damn it!

Viktor

I practically hung up on Tate when I saw Elaina all wispy-eyed talking to Spartak. I'm glad she appreciates his company but if I see them getting too close I will assign him to another detail and put my next best man with her. I know I should trust her, but it's in my blood not to trust anyone entirely.

Thankfully, my little trick at the bar worked. Since I made her a manager she should mainly be in the office and won't have to bartend unless someone doesn't show up. For me that means no more watching pathetic idiots checking her out on a daily basis. There have been plenty of times when I have wanted to sink one of those fools in the lake.

Enough of that, I need to prepare my love some dinner. I think she has it in her head that I don't know how to cook. Is it wrong of me that I almost want to pretend like I don't know how? That way she will make me a nice meal. I know she would, too. I probably wouldn't even have to ask her for it.

Opening the stainless steel refrigerator, I scan the contents. This may be a cabin, decorated to Mishka's standards, but I refuse to not have top of the line appliances. I have some stew meat and veggies, whipping cream, strawberries; I can definitely make something up with this.

Mishka must have sent some fresh foods up this week. I usually have a groundskeeper that helps maintain the place while I'm away. Luckily Mishka is sweet on him so she sends up fresh foods frequently. He'll enjoy having the next few days off and I'll have peace of mind knowing Elaina is safe with me.

I'm preparing a nice stew for the main dish with fresh baked bread my grandmother made recently. The strawberries and fresh whipping cream will go splendid afterwards. I hope Elaina enjoys it.

I didn't even stop to think about asking what foods she likes to eat. I see her sneak a cherry or orange at the club occasionally, and I've seen her eat at my brother's a few times, but she just picked at her food.

I grab the bottle of vodka from the freezer, pouring half a tumbler full and gulping down a good portion of it. I can't even fathom the fact that I'm nervous right now. Since when does Viktor Masterson get nervous over anything? Well, other than making sure Elaina is protected. There was the time I was at lunch and also when she freaked out at her apartment. Christ, maybe she really does make me nervous.

"Viktor?" Elaina calls hesitantly and I spin around to face her.

"Yes, Printsyessa?" (Princess)

"Are you cooking right now or is someone here?" She walks into the kitchen glancing over everything nosily. She's never been much of a curious cat, more standoffish than anything. This new side she's showing me is quite amusing.

"Of course it's me, why is it so strange to believe the idea of me cooking? Surely you must know that men cook."

Rolling her eyes, she huffs, "Of course I know that men cook! You on the other hand, not so much. You bring food to eat, like, every single shift I work. Naturally I would think you don't cook."

"Well for you, Elaina, I cook," I rasp and she blushes slightly.

"What are you making anyhow? It smells fantastic."

"I'm making a beef stew, is that alright with you?"

"Oh yes, I love it!"

I nod and she peeks over my shoulder as I take the chilled bowl and beaters out of the freezer.

"What are you making now?"

"Whipping cream. Hand me the sugar." I gesture to the canister and she quickly complies.

She bumps her elbow into mine several times while I'm mixing, sending heat through my body with each small caress. She does it again for probably the ninth time and I feel like slamming her into a wall.

I growl, frustrated, and toss the beaters into the sink, then grasp her arm, pulling her close. Elaina jumps as I grab her and I chuckle. "Oh, little lamb, you have no clue how much of a wolf I really am," I rasp, completely turned on by her soft touch, her sweet smile and flowery scent.

Trapping her between myself and the counter I reach past her while she stares at me, shocked and intrigued. Swiping up a dollop of whipped cream, I smear it down the side of her throat.

I bend down, following my finger with my tongue to clean up the fluffy, white sweetness. The sugary goodness melts in my mouth with each swipe of my warm, wet tongue. Elaina shivers as I get to the sensitive spot on her neck. Grinning, I take a small nip, just enough to make her jump a little and grasp tightly onto my shirt. I pull back slightly and she gazes at me, lost in a daze, I lean in and lightly nip at her bottom lip.

She stares at me longingly and whispers, "God, Viktor, the things you make me feel."

Turning slightly, she gets her own fluff of cream on her finger. She looks so sexy, I want to take her here on the counter. I study her as she returns the favor of smearing me with whipped cream, painting my lips and coating the tip of my pointer finger.

"Well, what's your plan, Princess?" I ask and swallow in anticipation.

She smiles and draws me down closer, sucking the cream off my lips. "Umm, Elaina," I growl. Picking up my hand, she sucks my finger deep into her mouth making me instantly picture my dick in there instead.

I quickly yank my finger out.

Shocked, she pants, "What? What did I do?"

"Just, let's just eat dinner, okay?" I mumble and she nods reluctantly.

I watch her swinging her little ass as she walks toward the table and it's the last straw.

"Fuck it." I throw my kitchen towel on the counter and stalk toward her, spinning her quickly, then I lift her slightly and place her on the dining table. "I'm hungry, lovely, but for pussy, not fucking stew."

"What!" She gasps, taken by surprise and I push her back on the table, lifting her skirt.

"What happened to your panties?" I'm staring at her pussy lips, they're just waiting for me to suck on them.

"I-I didn't have clean ones, and the wet ones are in my purse. Geez, you just startled me." She giggles, resting her hand on her chest.

"Startled, huh? Hold on to the table."

"Huh?" I spin her over so her belly is resting on the table, her bare ass on display in front of me.

"Nothing, just hold still," I reply and land the first rough smack on her butt cheek.

"Ah! Viktor!"

"Louder!" I say and land another smack to her backside.

"Ouch! Are you crazy?"

Smack!

"You've lost your marbles, mister!"

Smack!

Her ass is nice and cherry so I rub it soothingly for a minute and then quickly insert my pointer finger that she was busy sucking on, deep inside her little cunt. Elaina inhales loudly and I'm elated to find her sopping wet, ready, and wanting me.

Taking my finger out, I suck her juices off my finger and wrench her legs apart.

"You're here for me. This pussy is all mine." I dip my head and take her tiny clit between my lips, sucking lightly. She squirms and I brace her legs tightly.

"Oh my gawd! That feels good!"

"Yeah? This is the best tasting cunt I've ever eaten out. You keep creaming like that and I'm going to burst in my pants."

I reach over to grab the white taper candle from the glass candle holder. Rolling the larger, rounded portion of it on her hungry pussy, I coat it in her wetness and insert it slowly into her opening.

"Oh my God! Viktor!"

"I'm not God, Printsyessa, even if you do feel like heaven." I play with her little kitty until she starts to tremble slightly with the pleasure. "You ready for my cock?"

"Yes, please," she pleads as I remove the candle. I unzip my trousers and push them down enough to pull my large, hard cock free.

"Are you sure you're ready this time?" I rub the head of my dick in her wetness, dipping my tip into her hole and pulling it away each time she pushes backwards to get more.

"Damn it, Viktor! Give it to me!" she demands. I grip her hip tight and drive swiftly inside, making her call out loudly.

"I thought you were ready? And now this tiny cunt grips me so tight, pulsing."

"I am, I was, just please, God, that feels so good." Elaina clutches the sides of the table as I push deep into her.

"Oh you sweet, sweet girl, this is one greedy little pussy you have here, lovely. I want to feel this cunt come all over me," I murmur and smack her ass sharply.

"Ouch! Fuck!" she chokes and her center begins to spasm around me. This is proof that she loves it rough. She's going to be so much fun to break in.

I lean over her, clutching a handful of hair and wrench her head back toward me. Leaning in closely to her ear, I growl, "Make this fucking cunt come, NOW," and thrust harshly into her multiple times.

Her legs spread as her pussy grips harder me with each ringing spasm flowing through her body. Her legs go crazy as she attempts to scale the table to take me deeper but I grip her hair tightly, holding her in place. She will move when I'm ready for her to move. Each little squirm makes my cock throb, antagonizing it to finish deep inside her.

"What did I say when we started this? Who are you here for?" I ask, my voice gravelly.

"Ahhh, you, Viktor, I'm here for you. Oh!" Elaina moans as I pick up my pace, rapidly slamming into her.

"That's right. Me. This. Is. MINE," I say harshly, emphasizing the words with each hot spurt of cum I squirt deep inside her. Her pussy gets really slick from our combined juices and I pump into her a few more times, making sure my cum gets as far in as possible.

I free my hand from gripping her hip to rub all around my cock that's still resting inside her. I collect our combined essence and lightly brush it all over her swollen kitty lips and clit. She squirms slightly, sending little zaps of pleasure through my body.

I need to make sure she's covered before I'm done. I want every inch of her to smell of me. Next time my cum will be painting those plump tits and slender neck. I pull back from the table, bringing her with me.

"Woah, that was awesome!" She smiles happily, standing in front of me.

"Good. Now get on your knees and clean me up."

"Excuse me?"

"Get on your knees, Elaina."

"Okay, geez, quit being so damn bossy." She grumbles about it but she complies.

"I want you to lick all of your cunt juice and cum off my cock." She nods and looks at me timidly.

I caress the smooth skin on her cheek and smile slightly. She looks so beautiful, perched on her knees with my cum dripping down her legs. I nudge her slightly and she takes me deep, licking all over my head and shaft. I clench my eyes closed at the amazing emotions she elicits inside me. Her delicate hand grips me tight, pumping as she cleans me off thoroughly.

"Good, lovely, now clean my nuts."

She sucks them into her warm, wet mouth one at a time, swirling her eager tongue around them repeatedly.

"Elaina, my princess. You are amazingly talented with that succulent tongue and mouth of yours. I'm going to spill again any minute if you keep it up like that."

She releases my nuts and starts to bob her head on my cock quickly, causing me to curl my toes. My ass cheeks flex, and I reach out to grip the table so I don't fall over. *Christ, she's amazing at this.* She gets a good rhythm going but I'm brought out of my reverie by a quick smack on my behind. I gape at her, flaring my nostrils as she repeats the action and I feel the first signs of my impending orgasm.

"Christ, *again!*" I groan.

Elaina tightly grips my ass cheek and lightly bites onto my cock as she bobs. I surrender to the need and pull back quickly, pumping my cock rapidly with my fist, causing my dick to shoot hot jets all over her pretty breasts.

Leaning in, I softly rub my cock in my cum, spreading it over her neck the best I can. "Absolutely breathtaking," I murmur and she blushes, looking to the ground from my praise.

"Can we clean up and then maybe lie down? Or at least I need to. I'm actually pretty worn out from all the drama."

"I apologize, truly, I wish it didn't happen. Yes, of course. You're not hungry? I promise it is edible." I reach down for her and help her stand. She grips my hands tight, getting her balance and smiling gratefully.

"No, not really, perhaps later?"

"I'll just turn the heat down to low and it'll stay warm for when your appetite appears."

"Sounds good, thank you."

Hurrying, I put everything away that's decorating the counters from my meal prep and grab her hand gently to guide her to the large suite with master bathroom. This may be a small cabin but I had to have a larger area to sleep and a nice sized bathroom. This cabin is meant to be for relaxing as well as a safe house. I refuse to not be comfortable while I'm staying.

She looks around in wonder and I use the extra time to gaze at her gorgeous features. "Viktor, this bedroom is gorgeous! In fact, this whole cabin is, but this room is amazing!" Elaina turns to me excitedly and I grin at her in return.

"I'm happy you approve. Later I need to show you where the safe rooms are located."

"Safe rooms? As in, plural?"

"Yes, Printsyessa, there is one in the kitchen and another that goes completely underneath the cabin. There are three secret doors, I'll show you after you rest up."

"That is so freaking awesome!" Her eyes light up with excitement and I chuckle. "I don't know if I'll be able to sleep now, I'll be busy trying to figure out where they are!" She makes her way to the bathroom and turns on the multi head shower.

"Ah love, I'll show you the world if you let me" I mumble under my breath. "Tomorrow, lovely," I call out and she glances at me with a smile. She's full of mischief; I'll probably catch her checking out the house later while I'm trying to sleep.

Elaina
Two hours later

I try to get comfy next to Viktor in his extremely comfortable bed, but continue to toss and turn, staring at everything in the room through the shadows. The fan spins quietly, I miss my fan in my apartment. It's old and loose so it makes a ton of noise, blanketing the late night silence. It's so irritating, I hate not falling right to sleep when I'm drained. When this happens at home I will get up and vacuum or something, but I'm sure Viktor and his men would not appreciate the gesture.

I keep wondering if someone will find us here. The events from earlier keep playing through my head, like a CD on repeat. Kendall was pretty pissed when she left and I would not put it past that ugly psycho to come creeping. I would never wish ill on anyone normally, but that bitch puts the *cray* in crazy.

Those safe rooms have continuously been on my mind since he brought them up. Is his life really so dangerous that he has to have not one but multiple safe rooms? I wonder what they look like. I've never seen one in real life before. I remember that movie *Panic Room*. I wonder if his are the same way and where they are. I want to get up and search for them *so* bad, but I don't know whether one of his guards will shoot me if they see me.

I carefully scoot out of bed, trying not to shake it or rouse Viktor. That man is knocked out, sleeping like the dead. I don't know how on earth he can sleep well with so much drama going on.

My feet hit the floor and relish the feel of the plush carpet. The rest of the house has hardwood floors, but in here it's creamy white, thick carpet. Perfect, it'll make it easier for me to creep out unnoticed.

I snatch up his grey button down business shirt and slip it on, fastening it up to the crest of my breasts. At least if he wakes up I can try to distract him with a little cleavage. I've barely given up my virginity and already I'm thinking like a pro.

I'll just head to the kitchen and check things out. He said there was one in there. This way I can at least pretend I'm hungry or something, but I mean really, who can eat at a time like this. I want chocolate and that's about it, anything else is just a waste of time. I'm shooting for pure carbs and sugar overload. I could use a good sugar coma to help me cope.

I slowly open the door just enough for me to sneak through it.

Thunk!

Ouch! Fuck! I stubbed my toe on the damn door trim. *Stupid cabin full of wood, ugh!* I can probably turn on a light but want to get past the hallway first. I silently make my way to the living room and click on one of the lamps resting on a sofa table.

I'm met with Alexei's cold, tired gaze. "Eek!" I let out a noisy screech and clutch my chest. "Shit, you gave me a heart attack!"

"Hmm." He grunts, unimpressed.

A door crashes open and footsteps come pounding down the hall. Viktor appears, disheveled, pointing his gun equipped with a fancy silencer, ready to shoot someone.

"Alexei, report," he gripes irritably.

"Yes, sir. Miss Harper here was sneaking through the living room, when she saw me and let out a yell." He glances at me harshly, and then looks back to Viktor.

I huff angrily going on the defense. "Oh bullshit! I wasn't sneaking, I turned on the light in the living room for heaven's sake! If I was sneaking, do you think I would have turned on a light?"

Viktor glares at Alexei like he's going to scalp him. "Seriously, Alexei? Give her a break, with the day she's had, of course my princess would get frightened easily."

I smirk at Viktor, practically ready to purr at his kind words. "Yes, I was simply out to get a glass of water," I reply snottily to Alexei.

Alexei turns away hastily and Viktor looks at me, perplexed. "Lovely, you have water on the bedside table."

He says it like a statement but I know it's really a question. It's a stupid test to see if I will tell him the truth. It irks me even more to know that he knows I'm lying.

"Ugh! Fine! Yes, I was sneaking, damn it. You told me about the safe rooms and that's all I can think about now! Technically that makes it your fault. I wasn't expecting Rambo here to be waiting in the shadows and cause me to stroke out in the middle of the living room!"

Alexei just shakes his head and Viktor gives a low chuckle. "Printsyessa, really? All this because you're a curious kitten? Come on and I'll show you, so we can put this nonsense behind us and go to sleep."

I pout, bastard just called me a freaking kitten in front of Alexei. Obviously, I am too tired to be dealing with these two if all I can think of is throwing a lamp at them.

"Nope, I'm over it. I'll just wait until tomorrow. Good night, gentlemen!" I grumble and stomp down the hallway.

Stupid comfortable bed. I huff as I fluff my pillow and straighten the blanket over me up to my chin. They have it freezing in here with the air conditioning running non-stop.

I mumble to myself, griping about men as I quickly fall into a deep sleep, not even feeling Viktor crawl into bed and pull me close.

Chapter 9

Three days later...

For the third day now, I'm awoken by the smell of bacon in the air. I never would have thought Viktor could cook like a boss. His grandmother surely taught him well. I think he knows that I was doubtful of his capabilities, so now he's going to the extreme and making me food every chance he gets. It's sweet really; helps make up for me getting annoyed by Alexei being a permanent fixture in the living room. I know he's just here for my safety, but it feels a little extreme at this point.

It's the third day I've been holed up in this cabin. It's not some vacation either. None of the guys will even let me go outside. I really would enjoy just walking down to the lake and taking a nice long dip.

This sweet little place is nestled right between a lake and a mountain. I still haven't found out where we are exactly. Every time I ask, I get the same reply, "We're in the mountains." If they say it one more time, I swear I will scream.

The door kicks open and Viktor approaches, complete with a tray full of my breakfast and a sweet smile.

"Wow, you didn't have to bring it. I could have come and sat at the table."

"I know but I didn't want to wake you, I was just going to leave it if you were still sleeping."

"Pah-leese, you are going to spoil me and fatten me up. I've done nothing but sleep late and eat for the past few days."

"There is nothing wrong with that. You work hard all the time. I've told you many times before that I'll take care of you. You're a princess and deserve to be treated as such."

"That's kind of you, Viktor, but we've discussed this. I can't just do nothing. I have to work and stay busy."

"Then discover what your passion is and do that instead."

"I have to figure out what it is first and even then, I won't just roll over and let you take care of me without pitching in."

"Christ, woman, why do you have to be so stubborn. I know you are independent and can take care of yourself. I'm the man, damn it. Let me do my job and give you what makes you happy."

"Fine, you want to make me happy? Then take me swimming in that beautiful, giant lake I can see from the back window."

Viktor rolls his eyes and clenches his jaw. "You know I can't do that."

"See, then it's settled. You can't give me a simple thing to make me happy, so don't expect me to change everything just because we slept together."

His eyes widen in anger and he throws the tray against the wall, scattering the food and dishes all over the wood and white carpet. "You are infuriating sometimes! Stubbornness will get you nowhere but killed!" He's growling as he storms out of the room, slamming the door behind him.

That jerk didn't even give me a chance to reply.

Tossing the thick comforter and soft sheet aside, I hastily climb out of bed and head for the bathroom. I better not go out there right now, or God knows I will throw something back at him. I know throwing stuff is not the way to a healthy relationship, but I have to keep him on his toes. Relationship. Hmmm, I guess that's what this is after all. It's been a little while now since we first met since we started being more intimate and we seem to be getting closer. Oh and there's the part where I was there when he killed someone.

I turn the water to scalding hot; I need a good scrubbing and it's been a little while since I scrubbed off my past. Now is a great time to do it too since I'm angry. I don't know if scouring oneself is really the way to go about this, but it's something I've always done and it seems to help me cope.

Climbing under the hot water I grit my teeth at the high temperature and influx of steam surrounding me. I scrub as fast as I can stopping only to wash my hair. I thoroughly rinse my hair and body off and then get back out. My skin burns bright red. It coats me in a false sense of comfort, as it is pain I feel and not creepy crawlies.

Even after so many years I still catch myself feeling fingertips running over me, sickly, unwanted. *I'm not that girl anymore.* He can't touch me anymore and I have to get it through my head. After witnessing Viktor pull that trigger, I really should trust him that Brent won't get me again.

Enough of this shit, it's too early to pour over these thoughts and feelings right now. I'll save it for later to worry about. I have a bone to pick with a spoiled Bratva king, I don't have time to be wasting in the shower or on my bullshit past.

I pull on a pair of comfy sweat pant material shorts, one of Viktor's plain undershirts and a pair of ankle socks. Might as well, all I've been doing is lounging around. I took some scissors to a few of Viktor's things and made them little person approved. He towers over my short self, but I refuse to not wear clean clothes the entire time I'm here.

Viktor's clothes are very formal and boring, but when he puts them on, he looks edible. I never thought I could be so attracted to a man in a suit, but he wears it with finesse. It's not just me who notices him, everyone does.

Thank goodness I was able to bring my giant purse with me. It holds my basic necessities like deodorant, mascara, an extra razor, mace in case someone makes me really angry, those types of things.

I dig through it until I find what I'm looking for at the very bottom. I put on a swipe of deodorant and a spritz of my body spray, I'm good to go. I should learn to keep a spare bra in here as well.

Maybe I'll get lucky and there will be bacon left. With Alexei and Viktor though, it usually goes really quickly. Perhaps I should bring my mace and try it out on Alexei? That could be entertaining and possibly open up the opportunity for me to swim. Definitely an option to consider and I chuckle as I make my way down the hallway.

Arriving in the kitchen, I'm met with Viktor on his phone at the dining table and Alexei MIA. Thank God, some alone time without the puppy, Alexei, following us around. Don't get me wrong, he's a good protector, can be nice sometimes, it's weird constantly having him sitting here up my butt when I'm so used to being alone at my apartment all the time. It was hard enough getting accustomed to Spartak following me around constantly, and that was nowhere near as serious as this is. I do think I would be happier and more accepting if it was Spartak in here constantly though. I should ask Viktor to switch them when I'm done being mad at him.

Glancing around, I notice the squeaky clean kitchen. What the hell! I can't believe he cleaned this kitchen so fast and there's no food. He's been stuffing me full of it and now that I'm actually hungry, it's gone! Definitely not helping his chances, I'm even crankier now. I'm going to turn into a hungry plus angry person; they call it a hangry person. *Yep, I'm hangry all right.*

Perching against the fridge I glare at Viktor with my arms crossed. This is his fault for treating me like a spoiled princess. Before, I wouldn't think twice about there not being breakfast. I'd just go ahead and make my own.

In fact, that's exactly what I'll do. I'll show him that I am perfectly capable of making my own and I've never needed to rely on a man before. Slamming each cabinet as I go, I search for everything I need to make myself a yummy breakfast.

After a few moments Viktor mumbles to the caller that he needs to get back to him and hangs up. I giggle inside because obviously my antics are working to distract him. That's what the ass gets for throwing food around. You don't mess with a woman's bacon, it's simply wrong.

I start whistling an Andy Griffith tune cheerfully to add to his punishment as I whisk some eggs. I can't stand whistling, so hopefully he has the same pet peeve and it drives him a little crazy. Geez, I guess we are in a real relationship. I always read about couples annoying their partners and I'm definitely trying to get on his nerves.

"Enough, my love." he says pleasantly and it pisses me off that he sounds so freaking delicious when he speaks Russian.

I wish he would say more things in Russian to me. He could have called me an angry bird for all I know, but I don't care. His language is beautiful and it makes me want to climb him like a tree.

I bang the pans around in the cabinet causing him to wince. "*Elaina,*" he chastises and I smirk.

Alexei comes tumbling in through the back door, breathing erratically. "Boss! The alarm was tripped, get in the safe room. Hurry!"

"Nonsense! I'm not going to hide away."

"Please, sir, take Miss Elaina and go. We need to see who is coming and I want you two safe."

"I don't like this one bit, but I'll go because I want her secure." Viktor jumps up, rushing toward me. Alexei nods at him and shoves me toward Viktor.

"Hey, asshole! I can walk myself, don't touch me," I yell angrily, snatching my arm away from him.

Viktor puts his arm around my back and brings me close to his chest, kissing the top of my head and corralling me to the tall pantry cabinet.

"We're getting snacks?" He shakes his head, moving a few cracker boxes around. Suddenly the pantry shelves suck backwards and a doorway appears. "Holy shit, that's so cool!" I chortle excitedly and he pulls me in with him.

It's dark just long enough to creep me out, then a dim light magically turns on. Confused, I glance around until I see the light switch next to Viktor. "I feel like we are in a spy movie right now. Why are you being so quiet, you're making me freaking nervous."

The safe room we're in is a box about four feet by four feet with plain concrete walls, plush carpet, vents, and bottled water. We are already really close, and with Viktor's size the room instantly feels smaller. Definitely not *Panic Room* level like I was expecting. I really hope I don't have to go to the bathroom. That would be a whole new level of embarrassment in front of him.

"Relax, Princess, I'm just thinking. When I have a lot running through my mind, I tend to get quiet."

"Well, you're quiet all the time, so you must have too much air up there." I gesture to his head and he smirks back at me.

"Christ, you're feisty when you get wound up. Are you always going to be like this? Even when we are old and grey? Will you be whistling and throwing items at me?"

I smile widely. "Last time I checked, you were throwing food at me, and who says we will be together when you're a rotten old man?"

He laughs softly, stepping in front of me. I look up, meeting his gorgeous hazel eyes that shine with amusement. He's so close I can smell his rich, clean scent enveloping me in warmth that gives my stomach happy flutters.

He leans in a little more and I gulp, he's so close I can feel his body heat. "Umm, what are you doing?" I question, tapping my fingers nervously on the sides of my thighs.

"Oh, Elaina, I'm settling this little temper tantrum you've been throwing all morning."

"We can't talk about this right now. Alexei was just in the kitchen and I really don't feel like having your guards jump in when it's convenient."

"Don't worry, they can't hear us. The room's completely soundproof to the kitchen. We are handling this now. I'm amused with your banging around the kitchen, but not with the sarcastic attitude. I won't tolerate others speaking to me like that." He places his hands on each side of my body against the wall, leaning in and effectively trapping me in front of him.

"I don't care what you will or will not tolerate, that's your problem, not mine. And just what exactly are you planning on doing to handle this?"

Viktor comes even closer, so his mouth is next to my ear. His warm, sweet breath brushes over me as he whispers, "I'm planning on fucking you *so* hard, that's how I'll handle you."

I draw in a quick breath. Viktor rarely swears and when he does it stands out even more so. His words make my pussy contract and I clasp my legs together tightly, imagining him fucking me savagely.

I've turned into quite the wanton hussy since he first had me. He's been 'breaking me in'—his words—ever since we arrived at the cabin. Frankly, I can't seem to get enough of it. He has my body responding to him as if it's his own.

"Hard fucking, huh? I wasn't aware you knew how to do that," I mutter in return, taunting him. He has fucked me awfully hard, but I'm going to poke the bear as much as possible in this sense, I know I will be the one benefitting from it. That's one thing about Vik, he's very satisfying.

Viktor lets loose a ferocious growl and drops to his haunches, ripping my shorts down my legs. Standing stock still, I watch him.

He rises up, hurriedly stripping his belt off and unbuttoning his pants.

"I should spank you for that mouth. I won't though, only because you know how to suck my cock so well. Shall I make you suck my cock until I cum all over that pretty face of yours?"

Reaching into his pants he frees his swollen member, pumping and squeezing it a few times until pre-cum gathers at the tip.

I roll my eyes, still playing the part to wind him up further; this is going to feel so good. "I'm not sucking your dick, you're lucky if I ever suck it again," I retort stubbornly.

His eyes widen in disbelief and he huffs. Moving close to me again, he grasps onto each thigh, effectively picking me up against the cold concrete wall. He lines his thick cock up to my little hole and pushes in wildly.

"Ahhh, Viktor!" I let loose a scream as he pumps into me roughly.

My back scrapes against the ridges in the concrete and I rip my nails down his shoulder blades. He wants it rough; I can give it back to him as well. He knows exactly what I need and I know just how to push him to get it.

"Good girl, I'm going to fuck this pussy so hard, every time I touch it afterwards it'll ache. You'll learn not to push me, Princess, or you'll deal with the consequences." He forces the words between gritted teeth and I squeeze my pussy as tight as I can around him. He glares at me, then slams his eyes closed as he pushes into me harshly, grinding himself against my clit.

I moan quietly as he brings his nose against mine, his lips lightly brushing over mine as he murmurs, "And if you want a diamond on that finger, then you will suck my cock and love every minute of it." Drawing my lip into his mouth he sucks and gently bites down.

It takes a few moments for his words to register, my eyes flashing to his in surprise. "Vik?" I start to question, but I'm cut off by him thrusting his tongue into my mouth, taking me for a rollercoaster ride with his earth shattering kiss.

He pulls back from my mouth leisurely, and pumps into my cunt with passion. "Shhh, Princess," he murmurs, grasping my ass cheeks tightly to keep his rhythm. He squeezes them forcefully making me moan louder and I swear I feel his dick throb inside me.

"You feel so good, please don't stop, I promise I'll suck your cock," I gasp between thrusts.

"I know that, love, and I'm going to fuck this little ass sometime too. I will own every single part of you, as you own me. God, I love you."

"Oh, keep talking like that, shit, I'm going to come."

"Good, Elaina, you come all over my big cock and I'll fill you up with my own cum. I want to watch it drip out of your cunt when I'm finished."

I call out loudly, climaxing at his words. My pussy squeezes him over and over and with each compression Viktor breaths out heavily.

"Please come, come in me, please," I beg and feel his cock start to pump his seed into me. He leans his forehead on my shoulder and breaths heavily while he shoots his cum deep.

I start to relax my body after a minute, sliding down so my feet are resting on the carpet once more. Viktor pulls back and I smile sweetly at him. He clenches his jaw then drops to his knees, pushing my legs apart.

Glancing down, confused, I see him studying my cum-covered pussy with pure lust. I feel it drip and try to clench my legs closed but he holds them steady. Meeting my irises, he quickly goes back to watching my pussy.

When I least expect it, he leans in, feasting on my cunt. He sucks and licks at the combined juices like a starved man. Shoving my hand into his wild hair I yank forcefully, attempting to hold on while I'm on this amazing ride known as his mouth.

"Holy shit, Viktor! My God, you're going to kill me!"

He thrusts two fingers into me deeply, curving them towards my belly. I bear down with the feeling of having to pee. "No, stop! I feel like I'm going to pee my pants!" I plead but he ignores me, sucking strongly on my clit.

Out of nowhere a mind-numbing orgasm hits me. I swear rockets and fireworks explode in the sky when it happens. I grasp onto him tight, attempting not to fall as I ride out the amazingly strong orgasm.

When the feelings finally subside and I feel as if I can once again open my eyes without a blinding light being there, I gasp, "What in the ever loving fuck was that?" I grasp my chest dramatically. "I've never in my life felt something like that!"

He shrugs nonchalantly and stands up, adjusting himself back to his perfect façade. I stand here, probably looking like I was just run over. Viktor on the other hand, with a few buttons and a tuck, returns to his normal orderly self. I don't understand how he can pull that off so flawlessly and have to admit I may be a little jealous.

"Well, that was new! Geez, we can definitely do that again," I chortle, grinning cheekily. "Can we head out there though, because I'm really hungry now."

"You should have eaten this morning," he chastises and I'm too satisfied at the moment to argue with him. If this is his plan for the future arguments we have, then I'm in for some incredible orgasms. I smirk and he shakes his head at me, exasperated.

I hear a weird snap noise and pause to concentrate. Viktor does the same and then shuffles over to the wall, putting his ear against it.

"What was that noise?"

"Shhh!" he whispers harshly and glares at me.

I swear, with his moods today, he needs to eat a freaking Snickers bar or something. I stick my tongue out at him and he turns away, focusing on the wall in front of him. The strange noise rings out several times. I can't figure out what it could possibly be, but Viktor appears stressed. His eyes crinkle in the corners and he wears a grim expression.

"Oh for heaven's sake! Just tell me what that noise is!" I whisper-yell, glaring back at him.

"It's gun shots okay. Now hush."

"Gun shots?! Holy shit! It sounds like there have been a lot. Are they going to find us?" I inquire on the cusp of freaking out.

"No, Elaina, we are in a safe room and I'm the only person who has the code to get in here. There are only two of my men who know where this room is anyhow. I believe the gun fire is probably coming from my men. They will shoot or be shot before they allow anyone in the house."

"I don't understand why anyone would want to shoot at each other anyhow," I gripe, picking the nail polish off my nails. I guess now would be a good time to get dressed.

I slip my shorts back on and pull the T-shirt over my head. Geez, when did I lose my shirt? I don't even remember him taking it off me. Good thing my head is attached or I would probably lose that too.

"SpeSHEETS (Hurry)," Viktor says to the wall.

"What conversation are you having with that concrete wall exactly?"

He turns to face me, not looking amused and cocks his left brow.

"I was saying to hurry up. I'm hoping whatever is happening out there is over quickly. It's been quiet now for," Viktor glances at his shiny silver watch on his left wrist, "ten minutes. I'm thinking I can go and see what's going on."

"You mean we."

"I'm sorry?"

"You said for *you* to go and check it out, but you meant to say *we* can check it out."

"No, I'm fairly certain I said it correctly. It's simple. I go check it out, and you stay in here, secure." His response is stern.

"I'm not staying trapped in this tiny box! You can take me willingly or as soon as you leave, I will leave on my own."

"Absolutely not! You don't have any kind of a weapon. You need to quit being stubborn and realize we are at war here. I won't have you out there getting injured, or even worse, killed!"

"Oh no? And what if there's a fire? You're so sure I'll be safe in here and all."

"A fire? What are you talking about? They are shooting, not starting fires."

"I'm aware of them shooting. But what if they kill everyone and then torch the cabin? My butt will not be locked in this box while the rest of the place goes up in flames!"

"Clearly you watch way too many movies."

"I'm going, Viktor," I huff at him, standing my ground.

"You know, I could lock you in here."

"And I could kill you in your sleep, looks like we both have decisions to make."

Viktor turns away, angrily grumbling to himself, pulling out his gun from his leg holster and meticulously screws on the silencer. That's one mean-looking weapon he totes around.

He glances at me shortly. "Coming?"
I smile and nod.

Chapter 10

Viktor

This woman is infuriating. I never cater to anyone else, but I need to make some adjustments if she's going to stay in my life. I don't know if she realizes just how serious I am about us being together. Ever since I first saw her, I knew she was made for me. Tate has his Emily and I have my Elaina.

I'm brought out of my thoughts as she bumps into my back. "Shhh!"

Elaina nods hurriedly and looks around the kitchen. I follow, taking stock of the broken glass and bullet holes everywhere. It looks like someone just stood outside the cabin and shot the place up.

The wind blows in, swaying the pale yellow curtains.

I gesture toward it all. "Be careful with the glass, I don't want you to cut your feet."

She stares at the glass riddled counters, lost in thought. Tears spill from her eyes and track down her cheeks.

"It's okay, Princess, come here," I utter softly, pulling her to me. She grasps my shirt and buries her head in my chest, crying silently. My poor love has been through enough this week as it is.

I have to figure out a way for this craziness to stop. She will break from it eventually and I will never move past that. I'm torn from my thoughts as a sharp pain slices from my head down through my body.

I drop my gun in shock and melt to the ground, staring in horror at Elaina. She gasps and scrambles backwards. Mouth gaping and wide eyed, she points behind me.

I feel wetness drip down over my forehead creeping towards my nose, and I touch it lightly. Pulling my hand away, I'm met with red fingers coated in my own blood. I stare at Elaina in a trance as she screams bloody murder.

In a fit of rage she dashes for my gun, raising it up in front of her, aiming it behind me. *What on earth is she aiming at?* Blinking a little of the fogginess away I watch as she yells, body jerking as she empties the clip into something behind me.

I turn slowly due to the wobbly feeling I have in my head. Lying face up on the ground behind me is a very dead Kendall, along with a large, bloody butcher knife. Confused and foggy, I consider Elaina again, and then everything goes black.

***

Elaina

"Alexeeeeeeeeei!" I wail as loud as possible. Rocking back and forth, weeping uncontrollably, I clasp Viktor to me tightly. The glass crinkles and stabs into my bare skin with each movement but I feel none of it. "Spartaaaaaaaaaaaak!" I scream between sobs and hiccups.

As soon as I saw Viktor close his eyes, I ran to him as quickly as possible. I shook and shook him, but he never opened his eyes. I can see and feel him breathing, but there's no telling just how bad the damage is to his head. *God, the blood. There's just so much blood.*

I glare, angrily yelling at Kendall's motionless body, "You evil, stupid bitch! I HATE you! How could you hurt him? He was mine! How could you?"

Coughing, I lean over and lay Viktor's head in my lap. "I'm sorry, my love, so fucking sorry, my God," I gasp to his unmoving body, tenderly running my hand over his soft, bloody hair.

"Alexeeeei! Please help him!" I call frantically, my crying hysterical. I wait, holding my heart in my hands and pray to any possible being out there that can help me.

After what feels like hours, Spartak rushes in the kitchen door. He scans the entire room until his eyes fall on us in the middle of the floor.

"Miss Elaina! Are you hurt?" he asks, rushing toward me only to stop abruptly when I raise my head, pointing the gun straight for him.

"Don't touch him," I growl savagely.

He raises his hands up in a placating gesture and takes a step backwards. "Woah! It's okay, it's just me, Spar. I'm here now, so you are safe. Let me check the boss."

"Where's Alexei?" I sniffle and keep the gun trained on him.

"He's outside doing perimeter and building checks. We weren't prepared for so many people to show up."

"Go get Alexei," I croak, my throat raw from screaming.

"Ma'am, please. I can take over and help now if you would let me."

"I SAID, go fucking get Alexei! I will not leave Viktor, end of discussion! Now!"

"Yes, of course, ma'am," He nods worriedly, quickly jumping up and rushing out the back door.

I'm so sad and angry inside I feel like I could shoot ten other people right now. Not that I can. I emptied the entire clip into that bitch, but no one else knows my weapon is spent.

Seconds later I hear Alexei shouting frantically, "Viktor is hurt? Where is he? What happened to him?"

I clear my throat, and then call out hoarsely, "In here, Alexei!"

I don't even get to finish with his name and he's already charging through the door. He turns white as a ghost when he sees Viktor lying on the ground, frozen.

"Put the fucking gun down, Miss, now." He grumbles and hastily makes his way to me, not even flinching as he passes my outstretched weapon. His accent is more pronounced, I'm assuming because he's stressed out. "Tell me what happened to him, damn it."

I draw in a deep breath and calm my tears, having to concentrate on explaining everything. "We came out of the safe room, there," I point towards the pantry door a few feet away.

"He was warning me about the glass everywhere, you know how he is." Alexei nods and I continue, "then out of nowhere blood pours down his forehead. When he fell to the ground I saw Kendall had that huge knife. I realized she had stabbed him in his head and when she went to stab him with the butcher knife again I shot her."

"You shot her? But why didn't the boss shoot her?"

"Because he was bleeding like crazy and on the ground! Look around you, there is blood all over the place!" I flail my arms violently in the direction towards the bloody mess. When he fell, his blood splattered and smeared everywhere around us. "Anyhow it doesn't matter who shot her, what matters is Viktor is hurt. You need to help him, please!"

He crouches down next to us feeling Viktor's pulse. "I understand your upset, but did you check his pulse?"

"Well no, he was unmoving and unresponsive, I just figured he needs to go to the hospital or he'll die from all this blood loss. I know he was breathing, I saw his chest rise, but he passed out and hit the floor. It has to be bad, right."

"Head wounds bleed a lot regardless. It looks like he needs some stitches. I'm calling one of the guys in who used to be a medic in the Russian military. Try to calm down a little, you will help him out more that way." I nod and stroke Viktor's cheek lovingly, not paying attention to anything he says passed the word medic.

I hope he will be okay. I have come to care for Viktor so much. Do I love him? Yes, absolutely. There's no doubt in my mind that I do, after the events that occurred today. Alexei pulls out his phone and I stare at him questioningly. I don't know who he would be calling at a time like this. It's hardly the time, and he needs to be concentrating on helping Viktor right now.

"I'm calling Dmitry. He's the one who can help."

I nod, wiping at my tears. Shit. I have blood all over my hands, I'm sure I just rubbed it all over my cheeks. I probably look the part of a psycho killer now. Zoning out, I don't pay any attention to what is said on the phone. I have Viktor's gun and as I stare at him, I vow to shoot anyone who hurts him. I lightly kiss his bloody forehead and whisper to him, promising, "You'll be okay, love."

"Oh shit! Boss?"

I'm pulled out of my reverie by an unfamiliar voice.

"Relax, mouse, it's Dmitry. He will help as much as he can."

"What's going on?" Dmitry inquires, coming to squat beside myself, Viktor, and Alexei.

Spartak stands in the doorway, concerned, but also ready to protect us in case something else goes wrong.

Glancing up, I mutter, "He won't wake up and his head is bleeding all over the place."

He shoots me a worried look with his whisky-colored eyes and nods, bending his head to look at Viktor. He reaches for him and I raise the gun.

"Easy, Miss. I'm just going to have a look. I have to see what's going on, so I can attempt to fix, yes?"

I look him over from top to bottom. He looks older than us, probably around forty and in great shape. He has short brown hair to match his sparkly, intelligent eyes and has a pleasant nature about him. He doesn't strike me as a threat so I lower the weapon and he scoots in to get a better look.

"Well, it appears as if the blood flow has had some time to slow down and start clotting. Head wounds bleed more than most anyhow, that's why it looks as if you butchered someone."

As soon as the word 'butcher' comes out of his mouth, I start to weep miserably again.

"You fucking idiot! The nutso over there used a fucking butcher knife on the boss. Mouse saw everything," Alexei growls angrily and Dmitry pales.

"I'm so sorry. I didn't mean it like that," he says to me, remorseful.

I choke up. "Please just fix him."

He goes straight to work gathering everything he needs and cleaning the area. I sit stationary and watch every move Dmitry makes. Thank God the blood has slowed down some. It's still bleeding but it's not pouring out like before.

My skin feels stiff and gross from the blood drying. My nails are grimy and caked with it but I refuse to leave him like this. Even if Vik has someone here to help, I'm staying next to him every single minute. A harsh scrubbing can wait.

Meeting my eyes Dmitry kindly says, "Hold him still. I have to put in a lot of little stitches and don't let his head fall backwards, keep it elevated so the blood will flow downward."

"Okay. Do you know if he will he wake up?"

"He will wake up after some rest. I think his body went into shock when he saw his own blood. It went into protection mode and had him pass out. It's actually fairly common when people see a larger amount of their own blood. The wound's not deep enough to do permanent damage to the brain area. Luckily, this was right over the skull, so it acted like a protective barrier. Now, if he wakes up and after a while doesn't seem to be himself, then we should take him to the Emergency Room. I'm confident this will suffice."

"Thank you." I show my appreciation and Alexei grunts in agreement.

"Please don't thank me yet. Wait until we see if it works. And Alexei, we need to get him on the couch or to a bed and put a pillow under his head."

"Okay, now?"

"Yes, now. He is all stitched up and the only other thing I can do is put ointment on the cut. I'll do that after we move him though."

"Okay, Doc, sounds good." Alexei gestures to Spartak to come help lift Viktor.

"You're a doctor?" I quiz Dmitry.

Alexei interrupts, "Yes, he's a great doctor. He went overseas to help tend to the soldiers over there with the war."

My eyes widen marginally. "Seriously? That is so kind of you."

He shakes his head sadly. "No, Miss, they are the ones who truly sacrifice. I just sew people up."

I squeeze his arm gently and follow Alexei and Spartak to Viktor's bedroom.

I race ahead of them to fix his pillow perfectly. They get him all settled and the doctor puts a thick coat of clear ointment on Victor's wound.

"Thank you all so much for helping him," I say as they start to leave the room.

"Are you going to watch him?" Alexei inquires, peering at me curiously.

"Yes, I will not leave him," I state, making a silent promise to myself and glancing back at Viktor for a brief second.

"Good, take a shower and wash up while you wait. If he wakes and you look like that, then we will have World War Three on our hands."

"I would rather just sit beside him."

Spartak grumbles at me. "No, Miss Elaina, please listen to Alexei about this."

Rolling my eyes, I turn away from them. "Okay, geez, but I'm shutting this door because I'm leaving the bathroom door open for him."

They all leave the room and I'm met with a loud silence when I shut the bedroom door.

I'm not sure exactly how I should do this. I can see a large portion of the room from the shower, but not the bed, which is where Viktor's lying. I'll set the gun on the counter, beside the shower. That way just in case I don't hear something and he needs me to protect him, I'll be able to jump out quickly and take care of it. I know the cabin is empty besides the guards and the area is supposed to be secure, but I can't help to be paranoid. We were just attacked for heaven's sake.

I strip him of his filthy shoes and unbutton his pale blue, blood-saturated shirt, attempting to make him comfortable without moving his body or head too much.

Using a wet washcloth, I do what I can to clean off his face for him.

Once I complete that task, I cover Viktor up with the soft, light sheet. Dipping down and gently kissing his cheek, I make my way to the bathroom to start the shower. God knows I need a strong scrubbing. Today's a completely new kind of dirty.

Chapter 11

Viktor
Five hours later

I'm awoken by movement next to me and a sharp pain shooting through my skull. Everything's a little fuzzy but from the sweet brown sugar smell I know it's her beside me.

Taking a deep breath, I open my eyes tiredly and glance at my princess. Elaina sleeps on her side curled into my body, with her hands clasped together tightly next to her chin. She's breathtakingly beautiful. She has no clue just how much I worship her. The gun rests beside her with the safety on. *Good girl.*

Reaching over to lightly touch her silk-like skin makes my head throb and I hiss through my teeth. I've got to see what's going on back there. I remember the pain, but I don't remember getting hit with anything. It was instant pain, sharp and stabbing. And blood. I remember lots of blood.

Bit by bit, I attempt to sit up, holding onto the bed as I fight the dizziness. Christ, what did I miss? *Oh no, the kitchen!* I have to check out the cabin. I don't know if we're secure and if everyone is okay. At least Elaina is here so I know she's okay.

Okay, let's try this again. I rise gradually, until finally I'm standing at my full height. *That only took ten minutes to accomplish.*

I arrive at the bathroom mirror and I have to admit, I'm not impressed. There is still quite a bit of dried blood on my face and my hair looks disgusting. I can't look like this, call me vain, but I pride myself on always looking my best. I can't believe she saw me looking so terrible.

I flip on the shower and strip the rest of my clothes. It appears Elaina was nice enough to undo all of my buttons and to remove my shoes for me. That's fortunate, because at this moment I don't know if I can bend over without falling or puking. I can't get over the fact that I didn't protect her. What kind of man am I, to not be able to keep her safe?

Stepping into the steam, and under the hot spray, I grit my teeth to keep from yelling at the pain on my head when the water hits it. My appearance will obviously have to wait, there is no way I can run my fingers through my hair with soap to wash whatever's going on back there. I'm going to look for a small mirror once I catch my bearings a little better and see what hurts so badly.

Clambering out of the large shower, I'm unamused at how ungraceful every action of mine seems to be. I feel like I'm an inexperienced toddler, banging around everywhere. I don't know if I'll even be able to get my clothes on successfully.

Leaning over the sink to brush my teeth, I catch a brief glimpse at a pile of clothes on the floor and do a double take. They are covered in blood. Not soaked, but it looks as if blood was smeared all over them. Surely that can't all be from me? If so, that would explain why I was so dizzy on waking up and especially after showering.

I didn't see any injuries on my lovely girl, though a lot of her was covered up in my t-shirt. I love that she steals my clothes to wear. I told Elaina to cut them all up or do whatever she wants to anything. I only care about a few suits, but even then I can always replace them.

Leaving the bathroom, I'm met with a sleepy Elaina sitting on the end of the bed. Her blonde hair is a complete mess, as if she fell asleep with it wet, and she looks absolutely adorable in her rumpled shirt. She rubs her eyes tiredly, not realizing I'm watching her.

"Princess, are you okay?" I rasp, standing in the doorway.

She gasps, head shooting up to look at me eagerly. "Me? Are you nuts? How are you feeling? I can't believe you took a shower already! You need to rest." She's rambling and I smirk. I adore the fact that she cares enough to chastise me and want to take care of me.

"Why is my pillowcase black and not the others?" I ask, puzzled.

"Oh, well, because of your head of course. I didn't want it to stain the light one with blood, so I changed it before the guys laid you down."

"Who laid me down? What exactly did I miss and what happened to my head?"

"Alexei and Spartak are the ones who laid you down with the doctor guy who works for you."

"Okay and what happened to my head? Why does it hurt so badly? The last thing I remember was a sharp pain, but it didn't feel like I was struck with something. I remember seeing you yell and that's about it."

Elaina's pretty blue eyes tear up and she stands, walking toward me timidly. "You were stabbed." She chokes brokenly, irises so full of sadness and fear. A tear trickles down her face and she glances away. "You lost a lot of blood and passed out. The doc sewed your head up and put cream on it."

"I see. So what happened? Who did it and are my men holding them?" Reaching out, I grab onto her hand, squeezing it to bring her some comfort. She seems so distraught. I know it was probably scary, but we're both okay.

Glancing up at me, more tears rain down over her cheeks.

"Princess, please. We are both alright. Stop crying and tell me, baby," I murmur.

"O-kay," she says brokenly. "K-k-ken-dall got in and sta-stabbed you with a big knife. You're lucky you're so tall compared to her or she could have seriously injured you. She was going to do it again, I swear. I saw her try to-to do it. I saw her rear back with the knife, aiming for your back, so I had to shoot her. I'm so sorry, Vik-Viktor. I promise I had to or Kendall would have hurt you more." She sobs and my insides mash together seeing her so torn.

Standing up straighter, I pull her to my chest, wrapping my arms around her tightly and whispering, "It's okay, lovely, you did the right thing."

Rearing back, Elaina glares at me, incredulous. "The right thing? I killed someone! You can't just wash that off, Viktor! Trust me, I tried. I scrubbed so hard I bled in some places and yet it didn't help with the demons screaming at me inside."

She pulls away from me and perches on the edge of the bed.

"I can't believe I killed Kendall. I thought you were fucking dying. You wouldn't wake up and there was blood everywhere. You wouldn't open your eyes and I just wanted to kill her all over again for taking you away from me."

She buries her face in her palms and weeps. I'm lost. I've never felt remorse for a kill before. I've always just taken care of the job. I clean up messes and take care of the bad things my father or brother never wanted to touch.

I step close to her. "Then why, Princess? Why on earth would you do such a thing if you are to feel so guilty afterwards?"

Glancing up at me through her fingers. "Why, Viktor?" She stands abruptly, putting her hands to her sides, face swollen from her weeping. "Because I love you. I would kill a hundred people to protect you, even if it makes me a completely horrible person. If it comes down to you or someone else, I will always kill for you." She sniffles and wipes her face, looking at the ground, obviously ashamed for admitting that she would kill again.

Placing my hand on her cheek, I tip her head to meet my eyes. "I love you, so much. Vee oo moy dooSHAA (you have my soul)," I whisper and bend to delicately touch my lips to hers. The kiss evolves from sweet to possessive where I own her mouth. Elaina submits, grasping my sides and returning the kiss with pure love.

Leisurely I pull away, resting my forehead on hers. My heart sings inside knowing that finally she loves me as well. I lightly run my pointer finger over her bottom lip. I wish I could make love to her right now, but I can't. I'm so wobbly and I have to take care of the pressing issues.

She mumbles sadly, "I killed someone."

"Elaina, I'm so sorry this is upsetting you so much, but to be frank with you, I've killed many bad people. You did it to protect me and out of self-defense. I'm positive after she killed me, Kendall would have come after you next. She never would have let us happily be together, or let me be with anyone for that matter," I say sternly, determined to get her to let some of the guilt go.

She nods, but I don't fully believe her. I pray she can move past this and find some peace. I'm not even going to blink twice at it.

"Come, little love, I need to touch base with my men. I've been indisposed for too long."

I eventually locate my cell and send a mass text so everyone can meet us in the living room. I'm too worn out to hunt everyone down. Elaina puts more clothes on, as do I with her help and we head out there to speak with everyone.

"Boss, glad you are doing better, sir." Alexei greets me as we sit down on one of the comfortable sofas. He sends Elaina a concerned look. I squeeze her hand tightly to help ease her discomfort and show her support.

"Thank you. Now where is everyone?" I scan the room, missing two of my men that I had sent messages to.

"Anatoli and Mikahel didn't make it, sir." Alexei delivers this news solemnly.

"Christ!" I snatch up the lamp from the sofa table beside us and throw it hard, shattering it against the wall. Elaina jumps but my men don't even glance at it. They are so used to my temper that the little outburst doesn't affect them.

"Calm, lovely," I murmur afterwards and she clasps my other hand tightly. Surprisingly, her touch soothes me and I sit back, cataloging all the thoughts racing around inside my head.

"Okay, first off, where is Kendall?"

"Boss, the Missus is in here." Spartak speaks up and gestures toward Elaina.

"I am fully aware of who is in this room. I'm the one who called you here, in fact. Elaina is mine. You shall treat her as boss, as you do me. Is that understood?" I say sternly and everyone nods their acceptance, looking at Elaina with a higher form of respect.

"Now, I'm sorry to hear about our men. I will take care of their families accordingly. That being said, where is Kendall?"

Spartak glances at Elaina nervously then toward me. "I had a few of the guys put her in the barn. I thought you may return her to her father as a show of good faith."

Surprised, I nod, pleased at Spartak. "Yes, that's very good. I will contact her father and see if there is any way we can talk and reach an agreement. How many of our men were killed here?"

Alexei leans forward in his seat. "Fifteen. They came in with guns out and ready to shoot. We weren't ready."

"Someone round up the bodies and take them to Minska Funeral Home, while you're there check on how Sergei is doing. We may have one large funeral for all the families to pay their respects at once since there are so many. Clean this place up and get it secure again."

"Sir, I took care of that already. I wasn't sure how long you were going to be unavailable."

"Good work. I'll call Kendall's father and get back to you about how we're going to move forward." I attempt to stand up but have to sit back down.

Alexei reaches to help me stand and I swat him away. "I can do it!" I grumble and stand by myself. Slowly, but I do it.

"Come on, Princess," I say and hold my hand out for Elaina. She stands and eagerly accepts it again.

"Are you okay? Do you want anything while we are out here?"

"No, lovely, just to lie down, my head is bothering me."

Alexei steps forward with a tube, handing it to Elaina. "For the boss's wound. Doc said to apply it to the stitches and try to keep them soft for a few days. He also said not to wash the area, just rinse it for a few days."

She nods and eagerly takes the ointment. "Thanks, Alexei."

We take our leave and leisurely make our way back to the room. I can't walk too quickly or I get dizzy. I refuse to have my guys help me to my room when I am still able to do it myself. It doesn't matter how long it takes us, I'm too stubborn to give in.

I'm moody and exhausted when we get back to the bedroom. That's the first time my men have seen me look so unprofessional and I don't want to make it a habit. I should have had Elaina help me dress in my suit prior, instead of being so stubborn.

She squeezes my shoulder as I sit on the side of the bed. "You sure you don't want anything to eat or drink?"

"Not now, I still feel too nauseous. Perhaps later if my stomach settles some."

"You should just get some more rest then. I want you all better and you never get to just relax. You always have something going on or some kind of drama it seems. You must feel like you're going to explode inside with the copious amount of stress."

"I can't relax just yet, I have to call Kendall's father, Kristof Cheslokov."

"I understand, Viktor. Geez, I feel bad for him having to learn to spell that growing up."

I chuckle and dig through my pocket for my personal phone.

"Da (yes)."

"Kristof? This is Viktor Masterson."

"Mr. Masterson, what can I do for you?"

"I was hoping to meet to talk peaceful terms."

"That sounds like a wonderful idea."

"I have something that belongs to you."

"Is it well?"

"No, it has gone bad and perished."

"I see. Then perhaps you should bring very good terms with you."

"I have an offer I believe you will be pleased with."

"Very well."

"Three days at the dock?"

"Da."

I hang up and plug my phone into the charger.

"Well, lovely, that went surprisingly well and he took the news fairly easily."

"How in the world could he not care that his daughter is dead? I couldn't even imagine talking about it just now like you did."

"Kendall has given him many problems for a number of years now. She was always stirring up trouble with men, she was the type who enjoyed them fighting over her. Kendall even got her sister suspended from her boarding school because she was sending random guys there, saying it was time her sister became a woman. Kristof will probably miss her since it's his daughter, but I'm sure he is also relieved. He didn't have to be the one to kill her and now he will get a piece of my stuff like he has always wanted. If anyone has an issue it would be his wife, but if we meet terms then he will handle her."

"How do you know so much about Kendall?"

"Are you being jealous right now?" I smirk and she rolls her eyes at me.

"No, just wondering, you're like an encyclopedia on her life choices."

"Her father has always wanted me to marry her. He believed I could make Kendall settle down. She'd have money and of course he wanted an *in* at some of my territory."

"Ugh, sounds like that whole family has lost their marbles."

"Pretty much." I make a disgusted face and she smiles. I'm so thrilled to finally see her send me a genuine smile again.

"I had Kendall watched for a long period of time and had extensive background work completed on her. I've never wanted any part of that mess."

She yawns and quietly says, "Can we go back to bed? Now that you are okay, I feel drained. I had just fallen asleep when you woke up. After all of the chaos today I would like to just put this gooey stuff on your head, go to bed, then eat something when I wake up."

"Yes of course, Elaina, whatever makes you happy, though I'm not looking forward to you touching my head. It burns horribly."

"Dmitry left you a few Vicodin tablets in case you were too uncomfortable. I can get them for you, if you would like."

"No thank you, I will deal with it and just take a few Tylenol. I want to be alert not loopy just in case anything else pops off."

"You believe something else will happen?" Elaina utters, worried.

"Princess, I think we will be perfectly fine, it's just a precaution."

"Okay sounds good," she rushes to the bathroom and brings me two pills along with a glass of water.

"Thank you lovely. You're going to end up spoiling me, you know."

She skims over my face, looking at me compassionately, "you deserve it Viktor. Not only because of what happened, but also because of before. For months you have taken care of me, watching out, offering if I ever needed anything, I was blind. I'm sorry it took me so long to realize how wonderful you are."

"You think I'm wonderful, huh?"

"Really, that's all you heard?" She giggles and I pull her down onto the bed with me.

"I want to make love to you so badly," I rasp.

"I know, but you need to get better first. Please just rest. We have plenty of time to make up for lost time in the future."

"That sounds perfect."

She cuddles into me and I wrap my arm around her, holding her warm body securely next to mine.

Tipping her face up and meeting my eyes, she says quietly, almost bashfully, "I love you Viktor."

"Ah, baby, I love you too." I respond happily and Elaina gives me a chaste kiss on the mouth.

God, I can't wait to make love to her, to fuck her, to marry her, all of it. I love her more now than I ever have before. I can't believe she finally gave in and admitted to me that she loves me back. Hmm, I wonder if she will even want to marry me.

We have to discuss this work thing also if I'm not able to reach terms with Kristof. I swear if anyone tries to hurt her again, I won't hesitate, I will kill them in a moment's notice. Elaina deserves so much; I hope I can give it to her, while running the Bratva. I wonder what she thinks of it all.

"Princess, how do you feel about my life with it being so involved with the Bratva? Can you live with it?" I pry and get no response. "Princess?" I question louder.

"Hmmm?" she mumbles sleepily.

"Never mind, Elaina, get some rest, god knows you have worked for it."

"Love you, Vik."

"Love you, too."

No one's ever called me Vik before and I think I like it. My stomach clenches firmly with excitement each time she says it and I just want to squeeze her tight.

I hope she's lucky enough to sleep without her horrible dreams haunting her. I won't hold my breath though. Every night Elaina screams in her sleep; I shake her gently, hold her and do what I can to comfort her. There are even nights when she cries out and claws at her skin.

I don't believe she's aware of it as she never acts like any of it happened in the morning. Some days she looks so exhausted. In the past when she appeared tired and worn out, I always believed it was from her working late hours and partying. However, now I see the real reason is that she has this monster coming after her in the dark.

I wish I could go back and torture that scum, Tollfree, all over again for her. I would hurt him in many other excruciating ways. I know it's him Elaina dreams about. I know he still haunts her even long after he's dead.

Now she has this truck load of guilt dogging her as well. I can only imagine what horrific things she will dream of now. My poor love. I will continue to love her and hold her tight. I will do everything I can to protect her, even if it is only from her dreams. It's my job now to make sure she's okay.

Chapter 12

Elaina
Three days later

I perch my hip against the tan granite kitchen counter and cross my arms. "I'm pretty sure I'm going with you," I argue stubbornly. He's not going to get away with bribing me with bacon. I love it, but it doesn't help his case in any way right now.

"Why would I take you with me when I'm attempting to reach an agreement with the man whose daughter you killed?" He glares at me, irritated. Big bad Viktor isn't used to anyone arguing with him, well, news flash! I won't just lie down and take orders.

He sighs loudly and continues, "Not smart, Elaina. I want you here and kept out of sight. I won't be able to think clearly if you are there and can get hurt."

"I appreciate your concern, but I need to go."

"What do you mean you *need* to go? This is men's business."

"Oh, you pig. You seriously just went there?"

"I didn't mean it like that, Princess. I'm Russian, we just handle things differently. You Americans think everything has to be a discussion."

"Us Americans? My God, you just keep sounding worse today! Please, dig yourself a deeper hole."

"Look, you're not thinking about this rationally. There will be many angry men there with plenty of weapons. You could be shot at any moment."

"Viktor, I need to be able to look at her father and tell him I'm sorry. It may not mean much to him or you, but it's something I have to do."

"So I'm supposed to chance losing you completely, just because you have the need to apologize?" He looks at me incredulously.

Exasperated, I huff, "You won't lose me, geez!"

"Oh, you're damn right I won't lose you. I'm a very selfish man, Elaina. If something were to happen to you, I'd blow through that whole goddamn family to get my justice. Now is that a chance you really want to take? Because you know it's true. I will slaughter that entire family as if they were cattle."

I can't imagine the devastation it would bring to those who don't deserve it if that were to happen. I don't doubt Viktor's word at all, especially when he looks so determined. I refuse to be the cause of more pain like that for any family, so I relent.

"Fine, Viktor, I'll stay put. *But* you have to keep me updated. It can just be a text message with a smiley face or something. I just need to know you are okay as well. Every hour, you better send me something."

"Consider it done, lovely." He nods and steps closer to me.

"There are so many things I could do to you on this counter," he murmurs close to my ear.

Shoving bananas and spices over eagerly, he easily lifts me so my butt is resting on the counter and I'm almost the same height as he is. Leaning toward him, I nibble on his lip for a moment, causing him to groan in pleasure before I pull away. His breath is rich with coffee and a touch of mint.

Viktor's pupils dilate and bore into mine as he trails his fingers into the leg of my shorts. They were his sweats that I cut so there's plenty of room. His eyes widen when he finds me without my panties and he softly runs his fingers over my pussy lips. Each inch he gets closer to my opening I clench it, shuddering with need.

Grinning at me, he inserts a finger in me to his knuckle. It goes in smoothly as I'm soaked and ready for him. I tighten my pussy around it and Viktor purrs something in Russian.

He pushes my shorts over more, creating a larger opening. I salivate in anticipation of him shoving into me with his cock. I love when he's in a frenzy like this.

Viktor kisses sweetly down my jawline until he reaches my lips. Softly whispering over them, "You want my cock, Princess? This is one wet little pussy you have here." As soon as the word 'cock' leaves his mouth I moan breathlessly.

We are rudely interrupted by a throat clearing. "Um, excuse me, sir. It's time."

Viktor swiftly makes sure he's completely in front of me even though his guy is looking in the opposite direction.

"I'm coming," he rasps to the guard and I can't help but giggle with my mind resting in the gutter at the moment. When I start to laugh, he pushes his finger into me roughly and I gasp, instantly quieting.

"I apologize, Boss," the guy says and walks out of the room.

Viktor is practically hissing as turns to me. "I have to finish this later. I'm not happy about it, but I have no choice."

"Ugh, I wish you didn't have to go," I pout at him.

"I know, Printsyessa, me too." He gently pulls his finger out of my cunt, sending lightning bolts of pleasure throughout my body. Grinning, he sucks on his finger then kisses me chastely before walking off.

After I've had a few minutes to catch my breath, Spartak comes into the kitchen with a whole new set of plans.

"Hey, Miss Elaina."

"Hi, Spartak, what's going on?"

"The boss set a temporary code to the safe room under the house, so we get to hang out down there while they're gone."

"Okay, and why do you seem happy about that prospect? I've seen the other panic room, and trust me it's nothing to get excited about. Take it from me when I say you're not missing out." I make a crazy face and he chuckles.

"I've actually seen this one already. I got the tour, and it's really cool."

"What do you mean the tour?"

"It's under the cabin, and huge I might add. It's bigger than this place. The boss told me it runs the length of the cabin, all the way underground to the barn. It even has another secret door we can use if we ever need to escape that way."

"You're joking, right?" I'm a tad skeptical.

"No, I don't joke. I thought I was going to get shot the last time I tried to joke with Alexei." Shaking his head at that, he continues, "The boss is in charge though, so he has to have a few secure areas. This one just so happens to have a movie room."

"A freaking movie room?"

"Yep, I asked why and he said if he was trapped down there for days he would want to be comfortable."

"At this point, I shouldn't even be surprised." I shake my head and eat a piece of toast topped with butter and strawberry jelly.

"Do you want to take some snacks with us?" Spar questions and stares longingly at my toast.

"Why, did you not eat?" I mumble with my mouth full.

"No, ma'am, not since yesterday."

"Okay, we can definitely take some snacks and sodas." I grab up a few things and follow Spartak to this mysterious panic room.

Viktor

"Alexei, give me some specifics about the other day in the cabin. I know you've told me a few important details, but I want to go over everything so I have my facts straight. I spoke to my brother yesterday and informed him of what I was planning to do. Tate's not thrilled, but he said if we need any help to give him a call."

I shift more toward Alexei in the backseat, giving him my full attention as we speed in the Mercedes sedan toward the dock to meet Kristof. *Sail* by Awolnation thrums low from the Harman Kardon speakers.

"That's good, Boss. I believe I gave you the most important parts. Miss Elaina would be able to fill you in more about the actual act, if that's what you're wondering. I told you, we were all out in the yard and she was in the cabin, screaming hysterically until we came to help you. I thought she was going to end up killing us all when we tried to get near you." I grin at hearing my girl was protecting me fiercely and gesture for him to continue.

"I was wondering if Knees would be meeting us there, since Nikoli is close with Kendall's sister."

"No, Tate will stay out of it as much as he can. I knew Nikoli had a soft spot for her, but I didn't know it was that serious. Are they exclusive? And how do you know all of this?"

"I speak to him occasionally, and no, they aren't really serious yet, not that I know of."

"That could turn into an issue if Nikoli decides to get involved with the sister and becomes devoted. The last time he stormed into the club, it was because of Kendall running to her family and crying over Elaina fighting with her. I think he may want Sabrina more than you believe and he needs to be aligned with Tate's organization, not a female."

We're interrupted by Miesha, my driver. "Twenty minutes out, sir."

I meet his eyes in the rearview mirror and nod. Turning back to Alexei I have to refrain from rolling my eyes. I know how long it will take us, I own the damn buildings. I miss having Sergei here to drive me. All of this is Kendall's fault, she deserved to die.

Alexei clears his throat. "Let me speak to Niko before you talk it over with Knees please. I would like to make sure you have the correct facts about it all. I know Niko will tell me. If he's excited about a female, he likes to talk her up."

"I'll give you twenty-four hours," I murmur.

"Yes, sir."

The car stops and Miesha jumps out to scan the area prior to opening my door. He knocks on the window with his knuckles. Lev, my guard up front, gets out, performing another scan.

After a moment Alexei's door is opened and he gets out. They all walk around the vehicle to my door, that way they can surround me when I get out. It's the best way to protect myself from getting shot. They would have to hit a guard first and I would have a better chance at diving back inside the car or elsewhere for cover.

The docks over here are always dark and filled with filth. The air reeks of fish and old gas fumes from the boats. I'm fairly used to it, frequenting this area. Part of that dead fish smell is probably stink from all of the dead bodies I've watched sink around here.

"Watch your step, the rats are bad in this area."

Miesha looks at me with a horrified expression. "Rats, Boss?"

I huff at him, irritated. "Yes, rats, do you need Alexei to hold your hand or will you ask your balls to drop."

The men chuckle and Miesha turns away, embarrassed.

Alexei leans in closer. "Umm, Boss, did you pick a meet point? I would like a heads up."

"Yes, I discussed this with a few of the men yesterday. They've been checking the area since then and reporting to me regularly."

I hear Alexei grumble under his breath and shoot him a glare. He shuts up but keeps the bitter look on his face. We stick to the formation and carefully make our way to the meet point.

Kristof is patiently waiting, sitting in a black, standard folding metal chair. Three of his men surround him, and continuously scan the area, looking paranoid. When he sees us approach, he stands, extending his hand out of respect.

I shake it and one of his guys pushes a second metal chair forward. What a dirty place to have this sort of meeting. I glance around the battered building beside us and the trash on the ground.

"I'll stand." Kristof crosses his arms across his chest. He also stands, looking the part of an old man with his full head of silver hair. He's not as tall as I am, perhaps a few inches shorter. I'm more of a cut guy, not quite muscular but not small enough to be considered lean. Whereas he's slim, like he could use a few good meals in him to fill his clothes out properly.

I glance over at Kristof's men, scanning them from head to toe. He obviously doesn't care too much about what they wear. I firmly believe they are a direct link to the boss himself.

I always have my men dress decently. They may not all wear suits, but they're always in clean clothes that don't have rips and such in them. I don't pay quite as much attention to the street rats, but the guys I surround myself with, well, it's important and a requirement of the job.

Kristof's men look like hoodlums he found in an alley full of thugs. I wonder if he even provides them with any type of training. All of my men around me have been trained in hand-to-hand combat and weapons. I refuse to be surrounded by some waste of space who has no idea how to do his job.

"So how would you like to begin the negotiations?"

"Just like that, huh? You're not even going to pretend to be distraught over losing your daughter? You did receive her body?"

He nods, irritated. "Of course I received her body, you know this as well as I do. Why ask and have pleasantries? Let us get straight to business and leave Kendall out of this. Do I want revenge? Yes, of course, but I am aware that you did not want any of this. She started a war with the Russian Bratva who also happens to be the braat (brother) of the Big Boss of the Russkaya Mafiya. I'm not so blind and cocky as to think that there will not be consequences."

I'm pleasantly surprised at his rational thinking but not quite sure if I buy into it all.

"Kendall had one of my best men's throat slit, she put a bomb on my beloved's car, she had my cabin shot up, killing an additional two of my best men and last but not least, she stabbed me in the back of my head in an attempt to kill me. I'd say you and your family are getting off extremely light. I'm prepared to negotiate a small amount. Mind you, remember this is not compensation for her life, but a mutual agreement to keep peace once terms are reached."

He hisses angrily. "You don't think I deserve some sort of compensation?"

I chuckle menacingly. "You? Deserve compensation? You're joking, surely." He glares but shuts his mouth. "I'm the king of Bratva in America, perhaps I should demand more of what measly territory I allow you to have."

I snap my fingers and my other guards take a step out of the shadows. They stand like towers compared to the grease buckets here to protect Kristof. I had an additional ten men here waiting in case I needed assistance. All part of the plan I had discussed with them yesterday that Alexei threw a fit over. He may be my right-hand guy, but I don't run everything past him, it's the other way around. They all have to run things past me.

"What exactly is it you want, Mr. Masterson?" Kristof sighs and I know he's relenting.

"Well, how badly are you wanting to expand?"

"Very much so. I'm willing to do almost anything."

I rest my chin in my hand, thinking of what deal I can cook up that will benefit me. I had a plan in place but he seems to realize he's stuck and needs to be begging my forgiveness with this situation. This is exactly why I didn't want Elaina to come. He would have used her as leverage. Perhaps he would have played on her guilt, but it's not going to happen with me. My uncle taught me to be lethal when it comes to business.

"Kristof, I believe I have the perfect plan." I grin wolfishly. I know my ideas will frazzle him further.

"Okay, what is it you would like? Hopefully we can come to an agreement, I am a very reasonable man."

"I want a few things actually. First off, I want you to declare peace and call your goons off."

"Consider it done," he replies immediately, almost too eager.

I nod, pleased. "Secondly, your family and associates will stay out of all the clubs my family owns."

He blinks, confused for a moment, he doesn't know it, but it's to keep them far away from Elaina if she's at one of the clubs.

"Very well, is that it?"

"Not quite."

He looks at me questioningly. "Number three?"

"You always wished for Kendall to marry me, yes?"

"You were my top choice, you know this. I offered her many times to you. Perhaps all of this could have been avoided if you had taken me up on my offer in the first place."

"Good, then this should please you. And I wasn't ready for marriage at that time. Kendall would have been nothing but trouble for me. You were simply trying to push your burden off onto someone else. Anyhow, now I need your younger daughter."

His eyes widen and he chokes. "What do you mean you *need* her?"

"Exactly that. You send her to me and she doesn't ever go home. She will belong to me from here on out. Maybe after time if she does well, then she can visit you."

"So, let me get this straight, you're basically asking me to sell my daughter to you?"

"She's not for me. One of the men wants her. And yes, you will be trading her for your precious new territories."

"NeekaagDAA (never)!"

As soon as he spits the word out, I draw my weapon and swiftly put a bullet through the head of the thug closest to him. It makes little noise with my high grade silencer attached, but enough that Kristof stands gaping as his guard drops to the ground, motionless.

I gesture to one of my guys, Lev, to clean it up. My guard grabs him under the arm and drags him to the dock, smearing a little trail of blood as he goes.

Lev checks his surroundings, finally settling on a little bench. He secures the body to the small concrete bench then two more of my guys walk over to help him lift the bench and toss it into the water off the dock. Kristof's thug goes with it while Kristof gapes comically at the whole process.

Shrugging, I turn back to a shocked Kristof. "That's no problem, Kristof. If we can't reach an agreement then perhaps I should just start killing off people." I smirk and he cringes.

"No. No. No, now don't get hasty," he sputters and I'm pleased he can see I'm serious. "What do you want my daughter for? You won't be selling her to anyone else, right?"

"I won't sell her. I imagine she will be kept to be married."

"You don't plan to hurt her? No rape or torture, that sort of thing?"

"Christ. No. I don't get my rocks off by torturing young, helpless women. I got the Bratva here out of the sex trade for a reason. A person who works for my brother wants her. This will give you each a little of what you want. You can have warehouse E, which will expand your territory and the Russkaya Mafiya will get something that they want. The other terms are for me personally."

He eventually nods after a few moments. "I think that can be done."

"No, it's either done for sure, or not. You pack her up and send her over. You have a week. Then you will get the warehouse and I won't kill everyone you know."

He nods. "That should be feasible. I'll make it happen. Does that mean we will be at peace again?"

"It means we will be at peace when I have your daughter and I know you won't attempt to kidnap her back or anything. I'm warning you—and this is the only one you will get—do not cross myself or my family again."

"Yes, you have my word. If anyone attempts to cause trouble for your organization, I will personally see to it being handled in a manner you approve of."

"Then we have come to terms and have an agreement. This war ends." I am relieved, even though I hide it well. He nods and we shake hands again.

"Thank you."

I don't acknowledge his thanks, he's pathetic. We head for the car promptly, with my guards keeping watch the entire time.

We all load up and start on our journey back to the cabin. I forgot to text Elaina and I'm going to hear about that I'm sure. I'll have to come up with a creative way to make it up to her. I'm contemplating taking a nap when Alexei barges in right away about the deal I made.

"Boss, I thought I was going to talk to Nikoli first before you did anything with the girl."

"You can still discuss things with Niko. If he wants her then it will help keep her close. Then Nikoli gets a present that really cost me nothing; and I have an incentive for Kristof to stay on his toes. He doesn't know it but that warehouse is garbage and the State Troopers have been poking around it a lot lately."

"I understand that part, but what if Nikoli decides he doesn't want her, then what?"

"Then I will find another of my men to take her or she can become my house maid for all I care."

Lev speaks up. "Yeah, I've seen her. I'd take her if needed."

"There, see, she already has a contingency plan," I murmur and grin.

Alexei kicks the back of Lev's seat, "No. I will take her if Nikoli doesn't want her. I would get the first pick, right?"

Lev turns around and scowls. "You sound like whiny brat, Lexei. You probably wouldn't know what to do with that type of pussy."

"Enough!" I say sternly. "Look, Alexei, if he isn't happy with her then you may have her. I don't particularly care what happens as long as she is taken care of. No beating her or anything."

He grumbles and looks angry. "Of course I would never beat her or hurt her in any way."

"I'm not implying you would, I'm strictly putting it out there. Many men have it in their heads that when a woman is bought or sold that it's okay to treat her savagely. That is not the case; most women are actually sold to repay some sort of debt in the beginning. They should be treated decently, not inhumanly by a group of pigs."

He folds his arms over his chest grumpily and stares out his window. I guess that conversation is over with. I raise my eyebrow at Lev and he turns back around in his seat, watching the road.

Pulling out my cell I quickly type out a small message to my beautiful Elaina.

Me: I miss you.
Princess: You are in trouble!
Me: We will talk soon.
Princess: XXX

I watch the scenery as we make the trip back. It's so beautiful around this area. I hope Elaina will want to stay here or somewhere close. I love the warmth. Russia was always too cold for me, it made my bones feel brittle.

Chapter 13

Lev opens my door when we arrive, eager to speak to me. "So, Boss, does this mean you will get each of us a wife?"

I give him a look that says, 'you have to be joking' and shake my head.

"I'm sure you could find some girls cheap," he says stupidly and I have to restrain myself from punching him.

"No, if you remember, I got out of that business. The deal today was done for a completely different reason than to just buy and sell women. Regardless, that's none of your business. You want a wife, then find one when you have some time off."

"Yes, Boss." He sounds irritated and Alexei gives him a Cheshire grin.

I don't know what it is with them, but every time they are around each other they egg the other one on. Unfortunately, it's quite a bit. There is no way I'm going to make a habit of buying wives for my men. This is all so I can keep Elaina safe, not some free for all. I despised it when I watched my uncle sell off women to be maids, wives, sex slaves or target practice. I had to sit by and watch for so long, but now that I'm in charge, I refuse to do the same.

Alexei comes up beside me, clearly thinking seriously about something. "Boss."

"Yes, Alexei, talk while we walk, I want to see my girl."

He nods and follows. "Umm, when are we getting Kristof's daughter?"

"You heard the same conversation I had with him. She will be here within a week."

"I was thinking that maybe you would like for me to stay with her here at the cabin for a while to see if her father tries to take her back. You have the safe rooms and everything, so we would be able to hide her pretty well."

"That's not a bad idea. But Alexei?"

"Yes, Boss?"

"What is it with you and this girl? Nikoli already stormed my club for her once. I need to know if you have a vested interest in her as well."

"No, sir. I would just like to keep things within your best interest."

"So you don't want her then?"

"No, sir. Well, yes I do, but not if Niko speaks for her prior." His cheeks tinge slightly and I wave the other guards off to the shop.

"I'll keep you informed on what is to happen with her."

"Okay, thanks, Boss," he says as he plops down on one of the sofas.

I continue walking and make my way down a small set of basement stairs off the hallway by my bedroom. It's dark and steep. The stairs are lined with rope lighting in case of an emergency. I would hate to end up falling down the stairs or breaking my ankle when I'm trying to get to safety.

They lead me to the larger safe room where Elaina is supposed to be. I can't help but feel excited at the prospect of seeing her, with each step I take bringing me closer to her. We haven't been apart much since everything happened at my house.

I can't wait to take her back there and have her belongings waiting. She doesn't know it but I had a few guards clear out her crappy little apartment and move her stuff to the house. Elaina will probably be a little upset that I did it without asking her, but she'll get over it eventually. I can't help it if I want to surround myself with her all the time.

I get through all the security features and eventually find her in the movie room. She and Spartak are in the movie chairs, wearing 3-D glasses while staring at the one hundred sixty inch screen and eating snacks. They are so caught up in the new Transformers movie they don't even notice me standing beside them.

I speak loudly and they jump. "How's it going?"

They both turn to me, Spartak a little pale and Elaina clasping her chest.

"Viktor! You scared the crap out of me! Spar, pause the movie please."

"Yes, ma'am." He pauses it, nods to me, and then heads for the bathroom.

"Having fun, lovely?"

"Yes, this movie is insane in 3-D."

Shrugging, I take Spartak's seat. "Eh, it wasn't as good as I thought it would be. I wanted more with the dinosaurs."

"Don't say anything! No spoilers allowed," she chastises me and I chuckle.

"So what's this I hear about being in trouble? Are you planning on punishing me?"

"Maybe, depends on how you are planning on making it up to me."

"Well, I was able to reach an agreement with Kendall's father. We still have to be careful for a little while, but I do have an idea I think you will like."

She smiles widely and raises her eyebrows. I had no idea she enjoyed surprises so much, I'll have to keep this in mind for the future.

"I was thinking that you keep mentioning that lake outside—" She squeals excitedly midway and jumps up. She starts to leave the room, but I interrupt her. "Elaina, what are you doing?"

She grins. "I was going to look for something to wear while we swim."

"Right now?"

"Yes, right now! I've been cooped up here and I'm ready to do some exploring."

I grumble, trying not to appear as if I'm pouting. "I have a feeling you're not talking about exploring my body."

She rolls her eyes and laughs a little. "Come on, *please.*"

"All right, you win." I huff at her and head for the door to enter the code. "Come on, Spartak!"

He rushes out quickly, his hair flat on one side. Surely he wasn't eavesdropping. I need to give him some time off.

We all shuffle out and head to the kitchen.

Elaina squeezes my hand and I realize I haven't kissed her since I've been home. As soon as we hit the water I'm getting a nice long kiss from her.

"So what should I wear?" she asks while chewing on her nail and looking up at me happily.

"Wear your black bra and a pair of my boxer shorts, it should cover enough." I will probably want to strangle each of my guards if they so much as glance at her, but I'll attempt to restrain myself. No promises, however.

Elaina

I'm so glad Viktor's back and taking me swimming. It's about damn time, I feel like I'm ready to go insane from being stuck inside. I'm not much of an outdoor kind of person, but the woods surrounding this place are gorgeous and I really want to check it out. Hopefully, we can come back some time to enjoy this place when we aren't trying to hide out from the world.

Once I'm dressed I head back to the kitchen with a bundle of towels for us. I don't like to dry off with the same towel I sit on. It may be a weird quirk or something but I feel like I'm wiping dirt all over me when I try to dry off.

It's bad enough my toenail polish is shot to shit. I didn't have any remover to fix them and when I tried to paint over the old, it made it look like I have some sort of toenail growth.

Viktor's on his phone as usual, but beside him are some sodas and sandwiches. I swear I'm going to gain twenty pounds by the time we leave here. I had thought I needed to feed this poor man when it's been the other way around. I've never had a man cook for me so much in my life.

He trails off telling someone to 'take care of it,' and I can't help but be nosey.

"What are you taking care of?" I inquire as soon as he hangs up.

"Would you like the truth or shall I make something up?"

"What? The truth of course! Always the truth!"

"Okay, I was having some of my men move your things over to the house."

"My things. As in, the stuff from my apartment? A few items or all of it?"

"Umm, yeah, that would be all of it." He's sheepish when he replies.

Viktor's normally so sure and goes for what he wants, not worrying about other's opinions. It's pretty amusing to see him a little uneasy about going behind my back and doing something that he knows could get him in hot water.

I pace around the kitchen, tapping my fingers against my thigh, looking him over closely. He clears his throat and stands up straighter. I almost giggle when he does it, but am able to hold myself back. This is nice, making him stress a little. I can't believe the fool didn't ask me.

"I guess I'll have to think about it, now let's go swimming." Viktor nods, swallowing and scooping up all the supplies he gathered. "Aren't you going to change?"

"No, I wasn't planning on it, why?"

"You're going to swim in your suit, seriously?"

"No, I swim naked," he declares quietly and I catch my breath.

"Oh! Okay then!" I quickly head out the back door but come to an abrupt stop when a giant man steps in front of me, making me gasp. "Eek! Shit, you scared me!"

"Vat are you doing?" he asks in a really deep voice, laced with a heavy Russian accent.

"Um," I mumble. I don't finish as Viktor's body presses against my back and he casually wraps his arm around my waist.

He barks loudly at the guy, "Lev! Back up."

"Yes, Boss." Lev nods and steps to the side. I don't know what that was all about but I don't want to wait and find out.

Swiftly walking down to the beautiful lake, I take in the fresh air. It's muggy being in Tennessee but as you get closer to the lake it's like the air seems fresher, perhaps because of the mountains. I know it definitely feels cooler than normal, surrounded by so many trees and being right next to the water. This would be a beautiful spot to camp if there weren't a cabin so close by. I wonder if I would be able to swim here every day when it's warm once things have calmed down.

The water is cool and refreshing as I dip my toes into it and walk a few steps in. Turning, I take in Viktor. He peels off his under shirt and I'm met with his glorious stomach. He's not over built like some men, leaner. He has the magnificent 'V' going on, leading straight to one of my favorite large places.

"Water's not too bad." I twirl my foot to create mini waves around me. I didn't swim much when I was growing up. I did everything I could to keep my clothes on, at all times.

"Good, I'll join you shortly." He sends me a grin and I answer him with a little smirk.

Shedding the undershirt I had worn down, I toss it next to him, drawing his attention again.

"I'm glad you're not naked, or I'd have to shoot someone, I'm sure of it," he grumbles and I laugh.

I head more into the water, relishing the coolness enveloping me. It's peaceful and relaxing.

"Come here, my lovely," I open my eyes and find Vik close by.

"Jesus, you're like a cat! I didn't even feel the water move!"

"That's because you're like a wet chicken, flapping around out here."

I glare at him and walk straight into his arms. "I'm not a damn wet chicken," I grumble and he chuckles.

"Are you warm enough, Elaina?"

"Yes, I'm good. I love it out here."

"Yes, so do I. It makes all the daily things go silent."

"We should swim more." I kiss his stubbly jaw line.

"I agree. So have you thought about staying with me? Well, it would be our place but you understand what I'm saying?"

"Why are you babbling? Is this making you nervous? Is it us living together? You know we don't have to. I'm perfectly fine going back to my apartment."

"It's not that. I'm not nervous. Ugh. I'm just... Well, I'm excited. I've never had a woman live with me, and now you are here. You are my love and I may have the chance to spend my life with you, to share a home, and it just makes me an incredibly happy man. I guess in a way I am nervous because you could always say no."

"Oh, Viktor, I love you, too. I would love for us to live together. After this week, I wasn't looking forward to us being separated anyway."

"Good, it is settled. Thank you."

"Wait, I do have a request though."

"What is it?"

"Is it possible for us to stay here?"

"Yes, we can stay longer and visit whenever you wish." He smiles and I shake my head. It's not what I meant.

"No, Viktor, can we stay here, as in move here?"

"Here at the cabin? But it's so small. We could make it bigger if you would like, or change it?"

"It's not small to me. It's perfect. I don't want to change any of it, well, except having the guards leave. This place feels like home to me. At least what I imagine a home would be like."

"Ah, it is Mishka. I wonder if that old lady did this so one day I would have love."

"Your grandmother? How would she know?"

"She always tells me my house is too sterile, that no woman wants to be cold. I never knew what she meant, but I think I get it now. Yes, Princess, we can stay wherever you want. I'm just happy you want to stay in the area."

"Yay! Thank you! And yes, this area is beautiful."

"Now kiss me, Moy lyooBOF (my love)."

So I do; I kiss him with every feeling of love I have inside me. I long for him to have all of me so I pour as much of my soul into it as possible. Viktor answers me with the same meaningful kiss. It's a kiss full of promises, of devotion, of happiness.

Viktor's sweet kiss turns more rushed as he relieves me of my clothes, tossing them toward the shore. He holds me tight, his skin setting mine on fire as he touches me. I dig my nails into his shoulders, silently asking him for more.

"Please, Viktor, I need you."

"I know, lovely, I want you too, so bad."

His sharp teeth nibble where my neck and shoulder meet as he gently pumps two digits into me. I clench my pussy tightly around them but then he moves them slightly, frustrating me so much that I grind myself on them, wanting more.

Running my hands over his smooth skin allows me to feel each dip and groove of muscle, his pebbled nipples, and his rippled abs until I reach his large cock. I grip it tight and pump quickly, trying to get him worked up enough to take me.

After a few minutes it works and he pulls my legs around his hips. After sliding swiftly inside me he moves, unhurried, making each pump delightful. God, he feels like heaven.

Viktor leans me back and feasts on my breasts, pulling each hard peak into his mouth and ruthlessly sucking on them. He holds my hip

143

firmly with one hand and lightly bites all around each nipple. With each nibble I clench snugly around his dick, making myself moan.

Tightening my grip on his shoulders, I pull myself up against him. His pecs brush deliciously over my nipples with each thrust.

Moaning "Harder!" into his ear makes him grip my side to the point of bruising.

"I've been too rough on you. You were a virgin and I have been tearing you up for the past week. I'm a selfish man. I should be being gentle; loving you, and not hurting you."

"No, please, I love it hard, I don't want you to stop," I plead while each drive of his dick sends my head into a whirlwind of pleasure. *Please don't change it up.* I love how rough he is.

"You will enjoy it soft, I promise."

Frustrated, I argue, "I love it when my pussy is sore all week long. I don't know if that's wrong of me, but each little twinge or pain I get, I remember you being there. I get these reminders all day of how well you loved me, of how much you wanted me."

He pushes into me slow and deep. I cry out quietly, enjoying the feeling of being completely filled.

"I always want you, Elaina, never doubt that. I love you and this body. Now shh, I'm making love to you." I bite my lip at his stern reprimand.

Sweetly, he kisses up and down my neck, murmuring in Russian, pausing only for little bites. He feels incredible. I'm just impatient and get so eager when we're like this.

Viktor's hands run tenderly over my body as I hold onto his neck. "I'll make sure you still feel me, love." He growls and pumps into me fully over and over. The water splashes in between us causing pleasurable little sensations all over my clit and anus, highlighting his movements.

I clutch him, my nails biting into his skin. All I can manage is to gasp, "God do I feel you"

"You feel me now, Princess?" He murmurs, repeating me.

"Yesss." I moan loudly as he drives into the hilt, gritting his teeth as he tries to prolong our pleasure.

Right when I start to feel my orgasm coming on I jerk him to me tighter and ravish his mouth with a crazy kiss. He grasps my hair tight, slowing me to control the kiss.

"Thank God you are mine," he whispers as my pussy clamps down on his large cock, milking him for everything he has.

He wraps me in a hug, burying his head in my neck and releasing his seed. My pussy spasms greedily, pulling each drop of it as far inside me as possible.

Chapter 14

Viktor
Two Weeks later

"Please explain this to me more. What do you mean we have to go to the house? We just got our things moved here to the cabin. We finally get everything calmed down and settled; now you want to change it up? What aren't you telling me here, Viktor?" Elaina asks. Her hand is propped on her hip and I groan inside. I know this isn't going to go over well.

When explaining things to Elaina, I *may* have left out everything with Kristof's daughter. I should have told her all about the trade but it didn't seem important at the time. We've had such a wonderful time together while moving into the cabin. We did change a few things around, but not too much.

Kristof ended up needing another week after his wife threatened to call the police. I guess his daughter—the one everybody is going so mad over—was supposedly betrothed to a member of some other Russian family. It's caused a big uproar on the wife's side of the family. I don't know the whole story and frankly I don't care.

I do know his extra week worked to my advantage with my princess, but it's also going to hurt me for not telling her sooner. She's probably going to go ballistic, so I need to figure out the right way to tell her how I traded a girl's life for a warehouse. However I spin it, she's going to have my balls.

Ever since I made love to her that day in the lake, she's pretty much ruled the roost. Elaina says we eat at a certain time or we have a certain color curtains, I've learned to step back and just nod my head. I want her happy and if these little things make her happy then that's the least I can do.

This however, I will probably be cast out to the barn for.

"Viktor?"

"Well, I didn't tell you absolutely everything that happened at the meeting with Kristof."

"I assumed you left some out, but what's so important that we have to move to another house for?"

"We have a guest coming to stay with us."

"Oh, cool is it someone from Russia? Or maybe your grandmother?"

"No, it's Kristof's younger daughter."

"Are you fucking kidding me right now? Her sister almost killed us!" she screeches, making me wince. "Why does she need to stay here? They don't have somewhere else for her to go?"

"It's not so simple." I close my eyes and take a deep breath. *When did I turn into a pansy?*

"So make it simple," she hisses.

"I kind of own her and she's coming because her father traded her." I swear I hear her growl when she hears my answer.

"You can't *own* another human being, Viktor. This isn't the eighteen hundreds or anything. Things don't work that way!"

"Yes, lovely, when you are in this lifestyle, they *do* work that way. Don't act so blind to my dealings, Elaina, you know what my family is, what I am."

"I can't do this, Viktor. I know all about you, but trading people? I have to draw a line somewhere. I just can't live with that. Does her mother know? My God, how could you do this?"

She sends me a heartbroken look and it makes me sick to my stomach. I walk to her to comfort her, but she backs away, and I bite my tongue to keep from getting angry. She shouldn't pull away from me, she has no reason to, and I'm not some atrocity she should fear.

"Please calm down, my love," I say quietly and reach for her again. Elaina turns away from me, disappointed, and I choke up as tears try to fill my eyes. It's the worst feeling; to have the person you adore and love the most be disappointed in you.

I can't possibly lose her, not now that I finally have her after all this time. I have to make her believe it's not my fault. Christ, I'm such a fool for making that deal. I should have known she wouldn't be able to handle that. The only way I can handle it, is knowing nothing bad will ever happen to the poor girl.

"Let me explain this further." I lean against the wall and place my head in my hands. I have to clarify this so I can dig my way out of this mess with her. "Kristof wanted to expand his territory and he is willing to do practically anything. The warehouse I have in a certain location has been being scoped by the Troopers and possibly the Feds so I needed to get out of it anyway. Kristof is a slime ball so this will kill two birds with one stone. As for his daughter—" She makes a noise and my eyes shoot to her just in time to see a tear trickle down the side of her face. "Love, please," I plead but she shakes her head so I continue. "On the way there to make the deal I was speaking with Alexei. I remembered that Nikoli was crazy about this girl. He was so over the moon with her that he stormed the club and tried to attack me for what happened between you and Kendall. I know that if I'm enemies with Kristof, then Tate will never let Nikoli and this girl be together; and it will be all because of me." I glance at her beautiful face again to see her watching me with curiosity, and I'm thankful her tears have dried up.

"So I told Alexei about it and he said he would talk to Niko and see what he could find out. When Kristof told me he would do anything, I knew if it wasn't to me, then he would eventually sell his daughter off to someone else. This way she will be kept safe, and have the things she will need. Kristof will have a reason to back off from myself and my family, and Nikoli gets a chance to have the woman he wants."

"So you will just give her to him? Just like that? What if she hates him?"

"Well, that's why we are going to the bigger house so I can see how she really feels around him. I'm not just going to throw her at him if she hates him. I would never do that to a woman."

"Okay," Elaina says quietly.

"Okay? Princess?"

"Yes, Viktor. Okay, she can come and stay. I'll forgive you for this. Just...don't trade people, Viktor, it's not something I can handle."

"Ah, thank you so much, my love!" I pull her to me finally and hold her tight. I breath in the sweet scent of her shampoo and relish the warmth from her body. I thank the stars for bringing her to me and allowing me to keep her.

"But if she tries to hurt us, I'll kill her too."

I try to refrain from chuckling, but can't help it. She's gone from protester to protector in a matter of minutes.

"Okay, but I'll kill her instead. You can't go through that load of grief again. I can take care of it."

I can't bear the thought of Elaina hurting inside from some ignorant person making a stupid decision. I don't know if she could even handle killing someone else unless it were life or death situation. Elaina is the warm to my cool; it gives us a nice, even balance.

"I have an idea, can I make a suggestion?"

"Of course, you are always welcome to."

"Okay, what if you bring them both here? There's practically another house in the barn. You could have them stay there to test things. Both would have everything they need, and you would be here to make sure she doesn't run off. It's a win-win for all of us. Have you spoken to Nikoli about any of it?"

"No, I haven't. Alexei is supposed to be handling that end of it and I was going to see how she felt once she came. I think your idea is really good, but what about my guards? Where would they sleep and eat?"

"You always tell me that expanding is not a problem. Why not get a few small campers or something. Plus they're portable if you ever need them somewhere else and they have AC/Heat/Stove/bed, that kind of thing. Plus you have that big shop out there if you need more room."

I lean down and pepper kisses all over her face, causing her to giggle. "You, lovely, are a genius! I never would have thought of all of that. I think it sounds perfect. I'll send a few men out and see what they can come up with."

"Awesome! And now I don't have to pack up our gorgeous cabin. Thank you, baby Jesus!"

"Elaina, you finally said it," I reply happily.

"What are you talking about?" she inquires quizzically.

"You called the cabin 'ours'." I smile wolfishly and she rolls her eyes.

"Oh my gawd, you're so silly about somethings. I have embraced that this is our home, happy?"

"Yes, I am, one hundred percent. I love you so much," I mumble against her mouth and she closes her eyes.

"I love you, Vik, with everything that I am," she answers and I kiss her tenderly.

Pulling back leisurely, she gets a panicked look on her features. "When is she coming?"

"Today, that's why I've been rushing you."

"Crap!" She jumps up and runs around.

"What? Why are you freaking out?"

"Because Viktor! We aren't ready!"

"Of course we're ready. There's nothing to prepare for, she's just a girl coming to stay."

"Shit! Men never understand this kind of thing! Tell whoever does the cleaning around here to get to washing the sheets for her bed!"

"My love, you've been the one zipping around cleaning stuff."

"Oh. Right." She scrunches up her nose, "Well then, I need to go clear out that barn and get it situated."

"Why don't I call the housekeeper who visits weekly? I'm sure she would enjoy the extra work time. Mishka will probably be up here again when she hears of another female staying."

"I can't wait, I love that mean old woman." She smiles fondly then gets that determined look on her face again, "Yes, the maid is a good idea. I'll go get started and you call her." She bolts right out the back door like a woman on a mission and I can't help but think about how amazing, and a little crazy, she is.

As soon as she leaves I slip my hand into my pocket. The box I pull out keeps feeling like it's burning a hole there. Flipping the lid open eagerly, I'm just glancing down at it when the screen door crashes open. I slam the lid closed, hiding the box behind my back.

Elaina peeks her head around and looks at me suspiciously. "What were you doing?"

"Nothing, I was just getting ready to make that call," I reply as nonchalantly as possible, my heart beating a million miles per minute.

She nods slowly. "Right, well, I was just going to ask you to ask your men to pick up some more sweet tea. We need tea if we are having company."

"We usually drink vodka." I shrug as I shove the box in my pocket as if it's my phone.

"Please get some tea."

"You got it, lovely."

"Thank you," Elaina croons, blowing me a kiss. She runs off to finish doing welcoming stuff and I breathe normally again.

I think she just gave me a miniature stroke by coming back early. *Let's try this again.*

I pull out the nondescript white box and flip it open. A stunning three carat, Princess cut diamond, shines brightly back at me. The plain Platinum band accents the nearly flawless diamond even more. Pulling it out carefully, I flip it over to read the inscription. Engraved in beautiful lettering is 'Прекрасная принцесса' (Lovely Princess). This ring was made just for her and it deserves to have her name in it always.

Elaina seems to favor more simplistic things. I have to come up with a good way to ask her. I don't want to be over the top and scare her, but I want her to remember it. I think I'll ask her tonight. She'll be so distracted with the company coming, she won't even realize what is happening until it occurs.

It's only been a month since we've been official, but I can't hold off any longer. It seems like I've wanted her for ages. We can have a long engagement if she would like, but this needs to happen sooner rather than later.

Elaina

I'm busy cleaning up the barn and trying to make it as presentable as possible when the maid comes in to relieve me. She thanked me graciously like I was the one who called her, so no telling what Viktor told her. He gives me way too much credit for things. I just give my input or complain about something and he acts like I hung the moon.

When I first met him I never could have imagined this would be my life, or that I could love him so much. I was so incredibly blind to not see what was waiting very patiently right in front of me. I could kick myself for holding out on him for so long.

I still have some setbacks with my touching issue. I've tried to let him know what triggers things and he has backed off a remarkable amount. He still shows me a huge amount of love and affection, he's just more aware of how he does it. I'm so lucky to have found someone so understanding of it all.

I used to think Emily was a little nutty with how she always acted with Tate, but I get it now. Emily's growing with Tate and I'm so proud of the woman she has become given all the stuff she has dealt with. Having a baby on the way has made her grow up so much and it seems like it's really good for her.

Now, onto seeing about Nikoli and this new chick coming to stay. Viktor calls it a visit, but I seriously doubt it will be short. I'm pretty wary about having someone from that family around here, and especially around Viktor. He doesn't believe I would kill her, but he doesn't realize how much Kendall changed me. I would never cause harm to anyone for pleasure, but best believe I would shoot this one in a heartbeat if it came down to it.

I hit up the shower to scrub this grime off and find something appropriate to wear.

I throw on some jeans, t-shirt and combat boots. Nothing fancy, I want to be prepared if this new girl gets wild and crazy. She's lucky I don't have a gun or I'd tuck it in my pants to look really bad ass.

I wonder if Viktor is aware what exactly he's getting into with me. I'm probably going to drive him to drink more than a normal Russian drinks vodka, and that's a lot.

Chatter comes from the living room so I silently make my way to see what's going on. Peeking around the corner ninja-like, I'm met with a gorgeous blond giant, also known as Nikoli, and a small sprite of a girl. She's dressed in skinny jeans, a plain tank top, flip flops and has short, brown hair in a pixie cut.

She comes up to Niko's chest—granted the man is like six foot four or something crazy—but I think this chick may be shorter than me and I'm short. They main thing that stands out though, is she is the exact opposite of Kendall.

We lock eyes and stare at each other for a few moments. She doesn't seem scared nor overly brave. I wish Vik would have told me her damn name.

Nikoli turns, catching a glimpse of me for the first time and beams a bright smile at me. He's freaking beautiful in a completely different way than Viktor.

"Elaina!" He gestures for me to come to him, holding his arms wide open. Of course he would be happy to see me, he loves my sister dearly and I look exactly like Emily. Well, besides the eye color. I don't think I've ever met a man so protective over females who don't belong to him.

Making my way leisurely into the living room and attempting to keep my features blank, I step to Viktor's side. I feel a large, warm hand grab onto mine and it's like instant relief. I have real live proof that he's right beside me and he's okay. Nothing like the last time will happen. I'll make sure of it.

His breath tickles my neck as he leans close enough to whisper, "Relax, lovely. Everything is going to be okay. You appear as if you've swallowed something sour. Please show them your sweet smile and be happy. I love you."

I briefly check him over then nod. "I love you, too," I murmur quietly. Inhaling a deep breath and attempting to look friendlier, I bend in to give Nikoli a brief hug. "Hi, Niko."

"Hi, little sister!"

"Geez, I'm not the little one! It's Emily, she's so stubborn sometimes. I'm going to look it up on our birth certificates; just so I can rub it in her face that I know I'm for sure older than her."

He chuckles and pulls the female in front of him slightly bringing her much closer to me. He nods to her proudly then introduces her, "This pixie girl is Sabrina." He grasps her shoulders, dwarfing her like a football player would. "Sabrina, this is Em's sister, Elaina. I told you about them all, yes?"

"Da, blondie," she answers half in Russian and I cock a brow. I'm not amused, she better bust out with the English.

Snotty attitude firmly in place, I prop my hand on my hip. "Excuse me?"

"I'm sorry, Niko likes to speak to me in Russian and it's become habit to just automatically answer him that way." Her voice is small and pleasant. She speaks kindly and it makes me feel like a tool for being bitchy, but her family doesn't like the man I love. It should be expected that I act wary around her.

Niko jumps in, razzing Viktor, "Never thought you would settle. This one must come with whip."

I giggle and Viktor shakes his head. "She doesn't need the whip, although I wouldn't exactly write the idea off completely." Niko busts out laughing and Sabrina smiles.

How on earth can she be so calm about all of this? She was just traded for a warehouse and she's acting like this is no big deal. I would be flipping my shit right now if I were in her shoes.

Hmmm, at least Sabrina is a better name than Kendall. I just met the chick five minutes ago so it'll take some time to warm up to her. I'll back off a little but she better not walk behind Viktor or I may go psycho. I do kind of feel bad for her besides the resentment I feel for her family. I can relate; I grew up with a family that didn't want me either.

Chapter 15

"Come on, Princess, let's show them where they will be staying. I'm sure Sabrina would like to get settled." Viktor carts me out the back door, Nikoli follows and Sabrina trails last. I sneak little looks back behind us a dozen times, paranoid there will be a blade in her hand at any moment.

I have to stop thinking that way. I just can't help my feelings; it's in my nature not to trust people. It's not a switch you can simply turn off and on when it's inconvenient.

I catch up quickly, whisper shouting, "Viktor! She's behind us! Let her go first!"

Viktor stops abruptly and catches me off guard. He shoots me an irritated look and then speaks over my head to Niko.

"You both head to the door and give me just a second with Elaina, please." It's not a real question, even though he makes it appear so. They smile and walk to the barn, waiting next to the door for us like this is totally natural.

He grumbles at me. "You need to stop this nonsense."

Glaring, I practically hiss back, "Nonsense? Have you lost your marbles? Her sister stabbed you in the back of the damn head! Your wound isn't even fully healed up yet and you want me to calm down? Not just no, but *hell no!*"

"Ugh, you're so infuriating sometimes! I know who she is! I was the one who was stabbed for Christ's sake!"

I know he's irritated but he just sends a friendly smile to Niko, like we're having a normal conversation about dinner or something. "If you give me two minutes I could tell you that she apologized profusely as soon as she came in the door and explained her sister had terrorized her. She's grateful because she thinks you helped her out but feels guilty because it was her sister. Her father has already told her that if she so much as screws this up with any of us that he will kill her himself. They are *not* a very caring family. I would assume you have a touch of compassion to share, being you were her advocate not too long ago when you found out about the trade."

"I'm not sure I buy it just yet. I just met her. You can't expect me to be buddies with her when I know nothing about her. And I gave you two minutes; in fact, you had two goddamn weeks." I finish my reprimand and stomp the rest of the way to the barn, painting a smile on my face.

I open the barn door so we can all go in and get our new 'guests' settled in comfortably. We will definitely be talking more about this crap.

Viktor catches up quickly, acting as if he didn't just get put in the doghouse. We show them around the ginormous building. If it wasn't for the safe room under the house, then this place would be bigger than the cabin. The barn actually resembles the cabin slightly, being that it's all wood. It's missing the porch, and the windows in here are fewer but much bigger.

The barn has been converted into more of a loft type space. Up the ladder there is a landing large enough to fit three full size beds for the guards. I had them take the stinky mattresses with them when they left though and asked Alexei to bring up a new large bed the same size as ours. It's a king size, which I'm now patting myself on the back for because otherwise Niko would have been hanging off the bed from the knees down.

I hung the old light blue curtains we had in the kitchen and used one of the new packaged comforters from the safe room downstairs. Being broke the majority of the time meant I never really had many options when it came to decorating. I may have gotten a little overexcited at the chance of sprucing up the barn.

Looking pleasantly surprised, Viktor's eyes shine with approval. It warms me inside to know he is proud of something I did, no matter how small.

The bathroom was a disaster. Thankfully, the cleaning lady gave it a good scrubbing and I brought new cream colored towels over from the cabin's guest bathroom. I love the huge fluffy towels we have.

The kitchen is a tiny space. It's adorned with a two-seater wooden table and was hard to do anything with, so it's still dreary. I did pick some pretty purple and orange wildflowers for the table though.

I can't believe I went to all this trouble to make them comfortable and it hadn't even registered until now. It didn't seem like I was preparing for an enemy, but for a guest instead. I guess because of Nikoli I have been treating this whole 'stay with us' issue as if they really are our guests.

At least Sabrina will be sleeping out here and we will be locked securely in the cabin, with Alexei as a watch dog. Hopefully, Niko will keep her in check, so I won't have to worry about it too much.

"Well, I hope you will be comfortable staying here," I direct to Niko.

"I will be very comfortable," he smirks cheekily towards Sabrina.

She glances at me a little unsure. "So, where's the other bed?"

"What do you mean? We showed you the bed up in the loft."

"I know that but there has to be another bed, right? I mean there's only one bed but there are two of us."

Niko jumps in. "No problem, I sleep on the floor. Unless you would want me to keep you warm at night."

I look around at the wooden floors crazily, then back at him. "Um, no. The floor's way too hard to sleep on! I thought you would be sharing or I would have had another bed set up. I'm so sorry. I just figured you know, since you are staying together and everything..."

Niko squeezes my arm gently causing Sabrina's eyes to shoot straight to the place he touched me.

"It's no problem. We will figure it all out."

"Are you sure, Nikoli?"

We can probably get another bed in here, maybe not tonight, but probably tomorrow.

Grabbing my hand, Viktor responds for him, "My love, they will figure it out. Come on, let's give them some time." Giving in, I nod. Screw it, why not; I've already gone out of my way when I don't even know the chick.

"All right. Well, the fridge is well stocked so help yourself." I head to the door and Sabrina follows.

"Look, Elaina, I just wanted to say thank you so much. You have no idea what you and Viktor have done for me. I don't know how to possibly repay you for it, but someday I hope I can."

Swallowing a large gulp, all I can do is nod with the sudden blockage in my throat. She clutches my hands in hers and gives them a firm squeeze before walking back over to Niko. He smiles at her as if she's the best glass of sweet tea he's ever had.

Score one for Sabrina. She completely blind-sided me with that one. Vik and Nikoli do a small handshake and say their goodnights. Sabrina squeezes Viktor's hands the same way as she had mine and looks at him gratefully.

Viktor

The barn situation was strange, and yet a success, I believe. Sabrina did the right thing to reach out to Elaina. I have to admit it took guts and it earned her a pinch of respect from me in that moment.

I already know where Nikoli stands with Sabrina without even speaking to him about it. One look at him and I can see it in his eyes. He has that same determined look I had when I first saw Elaina. I wish Sabrina good luck in fighting him.

I should let Alexei know his chance of having Sabrina is a lost cause. Nikoli is bull headed and very intelligent; he won't let her slip through his grasp. Alexei won't have a fighting chance if she even feels a smidge of that toward Niko in return.

We arrive back in the cabin and I try to think up stuff for Elaina to do so I can plan my surprise. I already informed the guys earlier of what my plans are and they are doing their tasks on that end. I called Mishka and she was sending stuff up as soon as possible. I've been thinking about this a little for a few days now, but I can't wait any longer for it. The rest is on me.

"Princess, go to the safe room please. We need a nice blanket, a few candles in jars and a lighter or matches."

"Oh, sounds fun! Okay, I'm game. I'll go see what I can come up with and bring it up here okay? Oh and can you think of what to do for dinner? I'm starting to get hungry."

"Sure, thanks love." Landing a chaste peck on her soft lips, I open the refrigerator to appear as if I'm looking for dinner.

She flashes me a soft smile and heads downstairs. As soon as the door leading downstairs closes I race around digging through the kitchen cabinets. Once I find a note pad and pen, I scribble 'Meet me at our swim spot. Love, Vik.'

Thank God my men already took everything down there to be set up. That's why it was so important to show Niko and Sabrina around the barn. Normally I wouldn't have done that but the guys needed time to get everything I need without Miss Nosey seeing it.

Quickly, I drop my pants, slip my shoes off, and deftly undo my zillion shirt buttons. I yank out the pair of swim shorts I had hidden in the kitchen cabinet with the pans while Elaina was in the shower. I tug them up speedily and slide my house shoes on that I also stuffed in the cabinet. Elaina would kill me if she knew they were in with the clean dishes.

I need to put the note somewhere she will see it. *Hmm*, I'll leave it on the stove and put her soft drink next to it. Hopefully, she notices it right away and doesn't go looking all over for me. That could be a disaster.

Dropping the note, I quietly sneak out the back door. The door makes a rather loud noise and I don't want her to freak out if she hears it. She'd probably run up here thinking Sabrina came over to slaughter us all.

In my excitement I practically run to the beach, making it in no time at all. I can't wait to see her expression when she arrives, and then again when it's time for dessert. She has no idea what's in store for her.

"Good?"

Spartak stops his task to approach me. "Yes, Boss, a few touch ups and it will all be finished. I'm happy for you, sir. She's a good fit for you." I shake his hand, bouncing with energy inside.

"Thank you, she is perfect. I don't know if I will even be able to eat."

Alexei walks over and smacks me lightly on my back. "You will be fine, Boss. You deal with criminals all the time, what's one little lady, yeah?"

"For being a little lady she's given you plenty of hell." I chortle at him, grinning.

"Da, that she has!" he chuckles and they efficiently finish setting up the beautiful table and dinner I had Mishka put together.

Mishka made us her famous жаркое and sent it up. It's one of my favorite dishes. It won over Emily to the family and I'm hoping Elaina enjoys it as much as her sister did that night.

I take it all in, the wonderful spicy aroma from the meat, freshly baked loaf of bread, and the buttery goodness coming from the veggies. I have a lovely red wine and also some tea if she'd prefer. For dessert we have Swiss truffles I had Alexei order especially for this occasion a few days ago and overnighted. Then a homemade pound cake with a decadent caramel glaze.

The small table is formally dressed in white linens. The votive candles are placed tastefully around and a small, beautiful arrangement of cut purple hydrangeas and pink peonies are placed to the side. I don't want anything besides the food between us.

I want to be able to reach out and caress her anytime the feeling to do so hits me. I hope she's pleased with it, as everything was planned for her. This is our special evening and I want to remember each moment I'm able to make her smile. This is only the beginning of many more days and nights that I hope to spoil her.

The guys plug in the strands of tiny twinkle lights and try to hide the extension cord. They eventually make their way back up to the campers and cabin, fixing the lights along the way.

This way she now has a path specifically leading her straight to me. The lights twinkle dimly, it's not dark enough for them to stand out just yet, but by the time dinner is over it should complement everything beautifully.

I have the ring hidden with our dessert platters. I don't plan to actually ask her over dessert, just thinking it will be a safe place until I'm ready. I can't believe I'm actually going to ask her to marry me.

"You did this for me?"

Chapter 16

Elaina looks stunning, as she always does in her white bikini with navy paisleys adorning it. I could ravish her now, but I have to hold off. I have a plan and want to stick to it. This is her night, so it all needs to be about her needs. Right now she needs to see that I love her completely.

"Christ, your beautiful," I utter. "Yes, I did this for you." I hold my hand out to her so she comes to me. Tucking her into me tightly, my eyes close at the feeling of her warmth. She feels like home. "Let's sit, my love, you said you were hungry earlier and the food is ready whenever you are."

The emotion shines in her eyes as she whispers, "Viktor, this is the most thoughtful thing anyone has ever done for me. Thank you."

"You're welcome, lovely," I murmur back and kiss the top of her hair, helping her into the chair.

She sits and takes the lids of the dishes off, her eyes growing wide at the delicious foods.

"My God, this looks amazing! Did you do this? When did you have the time?"

"I didn't. Mishka sent it up for us. She knew I wanted to have a dinner for you and she planned accordingly."

"Your grandmother is so awesome! I'll have to call and thank her tomorrow."

"She would enjoy that, now please dig in."

I load her plate up with some of each and do the same for myself. The meat is tender and flavorful. The bread is moist and I inhale the divine smell with each bite I take. I even finish the vegetables in a flourish, probably eager to get through the food portion of the night.

"Viktor, slow down, you're going to choke if you eat any faster!" Elaina laughs, amused with my shoveling.

"I guess I was hungrier than I thought." Shrugging and smiling sheepishly, I clear the food away to the small side table. I need to make room for dessert.

Setting the truffles directly in front of her she groans and it makes me chuckle. I knew she would love them. As soon as her hand reaches for one, I bat it away. "Oh no, I get to feed them to you."

"Really, you think you are fast enough to stop me from grabbing one?" She teases me and I laugh loudly.

"Shall we try it out and see?"

"Maybe, but I see more dishes over there. I want to know what's in them before I decide if I should eat all these truffles. I want you to have a fighting chance and all." Winking, she gestures at the other desserts.

"You're quite bossy, you know that, right?"

"Yes, and it's one of the things you love about me," she responds cheekily.

"It is, and there are many others."

Placing the cake on the table with two dessert plates and new forks, I automatically serve her a small slice and place a few truffles on her plate.

"One rule."

"Okay, shoot."

"The first taste of truffle comes from me. Then you can have free range."

"Now who's the bossy one? Okay, I'll play."

I moan as I pop a truffle in my mouth. These are so much richer and more decadent than I was expecting. No wonder they cost me a fortune. The flavor is intense and leaves you feeling as if you just had a chocolate induced orgasm.

"Hey! How's that fair? I want a bite!"

"You'll get your taste," I murmur as I lean in, nibbling on her bottom lip until she opens her mouth. I stroke her tongue with mine, sharing the rich chocolate taste still exploding through my mouth.

"Oh God," she groans through the kiss and returns it fervently as I linger a few moments more.

Unhurried, I pull back from her tender lips and playfully tap the tip of her nose with mine. She keeps her eyes closed for an instant longer, taking in the flavors. I'm finally met with dazed blue irises and a lazy smile.

"Wow."

"Yeah?"

"Oh yeah! That has to be the best chocolate, like, ever."

"I thought you meant the kiss," I retort, disgruntled.

Laughing, she backtracks. "I was talking about the kiss, I loved it, but the chocolate made it out of this world."

"I'm corrupted, Princess, I never promised to play fair."

She rolls her eyes. "You don't play fair, you make it impossible to say no to you!"

"Good. Would you like to take a swim?"

She nods, moaning as she takes her first real bite of truffle, "Oh my gawd! We need more of these!"

"I don't eat many sweets but those could end up being a bad habit if we have them around frequently."

Grinning, I hold her hand as we walk into the refreshing water.

"You're getting quite the tan for being a pale Russian."

"Christ, you just want me to spank you today. I'll take it as a compliment. It's your fault, dragging me down here every morning for a swim. I'm getting tanner and leaner; you sure you're not trying to turn me into an Italian?"

"Haha! No, of course not. I wouldn't dream of saying the 'I' word around a macho Russian man, and I'm not opposed to spanking." She giggles happily.

I truly delight in the fact that she's in such a good mood after all the drama earlier. It makes my plan seem even better and more feasible. She loved the chocolate, I just hope she loves the ring as much.

"I love you so much, Viktor, thank you for this. I never thought I would be able to rib you. You've always been so quiet and grouchy looking. I see now that it just takes time for you to let your guard down to anyone and I respect that."

"I love you, too."

***

After swimming for about an hour, I spread the large quilt on the ground that Elaina brought with her. Lighting some big candles, I place them all around us since the sun has set and the only real light is the little twinkle lights leading up to the cabin.

The moon peeks over the mountain and casts a beautiful, rippled reflection on the lake. It's the perfect setting. The temperature is warm but comfortable, our bellies are full and we've had so much fun spending the evening not worrying about anything else.

I pull my board shorts back on since I'm done swimming and have had time to dry off. I should probably start wearing shorts to swim in regularly since we have a female guest here. That could be an extremely awkward situation if we ever ran into each other and I was naked from swimming.

Elaina dries off and plops down on top of the blanket. She's still in her damp bikini, skin sun-kissed, hair dripping, and relaxed. She's soul crushingly beautiful when she's like this. So natural, I can't even comprehend how she believed she wasn't good enough or that she was impure.

"Are you going to join me?" she asks sweetly.

"Of course, let me get a few things."

I grab some more chocolates so I can feed a few of them to her. I've never really done that before but it sounds like a great idea. Sneaking the ring into my pocket so she doesn't see it, I head over and lie beside her on the blanket. Her scent surrounds me and I have to bite my tongue to try to keep my dick from getting hard.

Elaina

I can't think of a better way to end this evening than by Viktor making love to me on the beach. If he doesn't make the first move soon, I'll probably jump him and take him for myself.

Vik murmurs softly, "You know I love you with all of my soul, Printsyessa, right?"

Glancing over at him, intrigued, I nod slightly. "Yes, I like to believe that. I love you with all of me. I hope you already know that though."

He brushes my cheek fondly with the tips of his fingers and I close my eyes, delighting in the soothing sensations. "And you also know I think of being with you forever, right?"

My eyes spring open, gazing at his hazel irises. "I know. I want that too, that's why I agreed to move in with you."

"Good, then this won't come as too much of a shock then."

I perch up on my elbows, staring at him seriously. What is he talking about now? It better not be anything new to do with stuff in that meeting.

He stares at the blanket for a beat while his cheeks pink slightly. Reaching into his pocket he brings out that last thing I was ever expecting to see today. He opens his palm.

The diamond glints in the candlelight and I choke out a surprised gasp as tears gather in happiness. "Love?" I question.

"Yes," he says softly as a tear tracks down his cheek. "Please, Elaina? I don't think I can live my life without you." He bites his lip and I sniffle.

"I'm already yours, Viktor. I would be honored to be your wife as well."

He smiles brightly, his eyes shining with happiness and excitement. Crushing me in his arms, he kisses me as if his life depends on it. Eagerly I respond until he pulls away, and places the exquisite ring on my finger.

"Thank you, I love it!"

"I'm elated that you approve, and thank you for agreeing."

He takes a bite of the truffle and feeds me the other half. If this is any indication of how the future will be, then I'm going to be happy and probably overweight. He's right; I don't think I would be able to contain myself if we had these around all the time. His yummy cooking is bad enough, but in a good way.

Once I swallow it I push him down onto his back. I draw one of his small nipples into my mouth, flicking back and forth with my tongue until it pebbles.

I run my fingers over his hard stomach, grazing my nails lightly as I go until I get to his cock. He's as stiff as a rod, ready and excited. Freeing it from his shorts, I run my fingers over it several times, following his happy trail with my tongue, I take him into my mouth as far as possible.

He threads his fingers through my hair and flexes his leg muscles. I know he's trying desperately to hold back from slamming into my mouth. He loves my mouth. I run my tongue around the little ridge at the top of his dick and suck hard.

"Ah! Elaina!" He groans and I bob my head a few times before coming up.

Climbing over his muscular hips, I rest my swimsuit clad pussy on his bare cock. He sits up abruptly, yanking me to him and taking my mouth with his. I grind my pussy against him and he kisses me roughly.

Viktor unties the frilly bows on my hips, pulling the bottoms out of his way. My wet pussy rubs against his dick, greedily coating him from base to tip with my juices, but I'm left wanting more.

He pulls away from my mouth. "Fuck, baby, you trying to kill me tonight?"

"I just want you." I raise my eyebrow, and line him up with my hole.

I watch him swallow hard as I swivel my hips, circling my opening around the head of his cock. After a few moments of teasing, I slam down on him until he's fully seated.

"Christ," he calls out and clamps his eyes closed.

He grasps onto my shoulder and grinds himself against my clit. God, that feels amazing.

I bite onto his shoulder and moan, "Oh yes," into his skin.

"That's good, love, ride my cock just like that," he rasps.

Viktor wraps his arm around my back and flips me over so I'm lying flat on the ground. I shriek in surprise and giggle.

He kisses me tenderly across my jawline while pumping into me a few times. He pops his hips and my eyes roll back.

"Yes, don't stop!" I plead as my cunt hugs his large dick hungrily, ready to come.

"Forever, Princess," he grunts into my neck as he thrusts into me over and over.

"Forever," I reply loudly as my pussy spasms, draining me of every last drop of energy as I ride out the most satisfying orgasm.

He groans, clutching me tightly as he empties himself into me, sated and spent.

After a moment he pulls back, regarding me lovingly.

"You're going to be my wife."

I smirk. "Yep."

Chapter 17

Viktor
Six months later

"Hurry up, slow pokes!" Elaina yells at me, Spartak and Alexei. "I should leave you all here and just have Sabrina come with me!"

Grumbling, I shake my head. "No way, it's my brother's baby too. I don't care that you've become such good friends with Bina, I'm taking you."

"Well, the baby was born if you haven't noticed and y'all are standing around as if it's time for vodka or something!"

I may have taken Tate's advice and lightened up a little toward my guards. Spartak, Nikoli, Alexei and I have regular card games at the cabin and tend to end up drinking a little too much vodka occasionally. If Emily's feeling well enough, Tate even joins in. I'm still very much focused on my businesses and my way of life, but I have to admit it's a pleasant change to have people to share life with.

I grab a few snacks from the kitchen, I have a feeling this will end up being a long day.

"I was supposed to be there when she had the baby, not afterwards!" Elaina yells again and I roll my eyes. I hear the guys chuckle from the living room. They find it really amusing when she gets into a tiff like this. She usually ends up throwing some random object and I'm always the target.

"Coming, Princess! Relax, Emily will understand."

I head to the living room to find her nearly in tears, she's so upset. "Come on, lovely, I know you're mad but no one knew the baby would come so fast."

"I know, it's just...I wanted to be there for her. For once you know? I wanted to be one of the first people to see the baby; she's the newest member to our family."

"You still can be. Let's get there before everyone else, okay?"

She nods and the four of us load up into the Mercedes sedan.

When we eventually reach the hospital she jumps out and runs to the front desk, babbling a hundred miles a minute.

"Yes, ma'am, maternity is up on level four. You need to check in at the desk and they can let you see her."

"Thank you!" She glances at me excitedly and takes off for the elevator. We all trail behind her like a group of lost puppies. People probably think she's someone famous with two of us in suits, and Spar clad in all black with his combat pants and boots.

Mishka stands at the front desk, eagerly waiting to greet people and brag about her new great-grand baby. We each hug her warmly and she leads us straight to Emily's private suite. Nothing but the best for my brother's wife and baby, as expected.

I have to admit, at this moment I'm jealous. Emily rests, tired and proud, showing off her little baby for us all to see. I hope one day I can see Elaina wrapped in her robe, carefully holding our new baby.

Elaina

Emotion pours from me as I stare at my happy sister holding her sweet new bundle of joy. It feels as if it's taken ages for her to finally pop.

"Congratulations, little sister." I sit next to her on the hospital bed and kiss her cheek, "I'm so sorry I couldn't get here sooner, I feel terrible."

"It's not your fault, she came quickly. I thought Tate was going to break a few pairs of knees during the delivery. I can only imagine what the hospital staff would have thought if you had been here and started throwing things."

"Oh my gosh, what happened?"

"Not much, just a rude nurse who got snippy with me when I cussed. I mean, really? I was having a baby! Tate threatened to buy the hospital and have everyone fired. The doctor spazzed out and had the two head nurses on duty come in for the rest of the delivery. It was interesting to say the least," she explains.

"Wow, all that over cussing?" I look over the little bundle of blanket to see my new baby niece.

"Yeah, I don't know what her issue was, but that's what prompted it. I can't wait to just get out of here and take this little one home."

"I bet. Just ask the nurses if you need help with something though. When I had to stay here I met some really friendly, helpful people."

"I did too, just a bad experience this time. I promise I will ask for help. Would you like to hold your new niece?"

"Definitely!"

Emily places her into my arms; I gently bring her close to my chest. She's so tiny and perfect. Her hair's so light it looks white.

"Emily, she looks like a little sleeping angel! Look at that hair!" I say excitedly and glance at my sister.

"I know, Tate said the same thing. We decided to name her Mishka after his grandmother. We're going to call her Mishka Angel Masterson. Angel because she looks like one and because I know she has many watching over her."

"That's beautiful, Emily, I'm so happy for you."

"Thank you, now she just needs a little blonde haired cousin."

I glance over at Viktor and smile. "Yes, someday she will have one."

I'm cut off by loud laughing and excited voices outside the room. The door opens and sure enough London and Avery pile in. They both have windblown hair, sparkly eyes and bright smiles and are followed by big bikers.

London's excited voice carries through the room, "What's up, sexy ass bitches!"

I just laugh, typical London. God, I love these people.

Thank you and I hope you enjoyed Corrupted!

Stay up to date with Sapphire:

Website *www.authorsapphireknight.com*

Also by Sapphire

Oath Keepers MC Series

Exposed

Relinquish

Forsaken Control

Friction

Sweet Surrender – free short story

Oath Keepers MC Hybrid Series

Princess

Love and Obey – free short story

Daydream

Baby

Chevelle

Cherry

Heathen

(next book coming fall 2021)

Russkaya Mafiya Series

Secrets

Corrupted

Corrupted Counterparts – free short story

Unwanted Sacrifices

Undercover Intentions

Dirty Down South Series

Freight Train

3 Times the Heat

2 Times the Bliss

The Vendetti Famiglia

The Vendetti Empire - part 1

The Vendetti Queen - part 2

The Vendetti Seven – part 3

The Vendetti Coward – part 4

Harvard Academy Elite

Little White Lies

Ugly Dark Truth

Royal Bastards MC Texas

Opposites Attract

Kings of Carnage MC Series

Bash – Vice President

Sterling - Prospect

The Chicago Crew

Gangster

Mad Max

Complete Standalones

Gangster

Unexpected Forfeit

The Main Event – free short story

Oath Keepers MC Collection

Russian Roulette

Tease – Short Story Collection

Oath Keepers MC Hybrid Collection

Vendetti Duet

Harvard Academy Elite

Viking - free newsletter short story

Dirty Down South Collection

Enjoy this sneak peak into my dark mafia romance series the Vendetti Famiglia.

The Vendetti Empire

Matteo

He gurgles as I strangle him—my hands clutched tightly around his neck, his face changing colors. First, it goes pale turning into an angry red; he clutches tightly to my wrists for a moment longer. His coloring switches into a purplish-blue and his meaty fingers fall away. Mine remain sturdy, a deathly vice until the fight escapes him completely. His weight grows heavier and I release, letting him fall to the floor, spent.

Another one dead.

Another traitor gone.

This is what you do when you're in line to be Capo. You clean house as the time nears to take the reins. My father's old, and he wants to retire. He deserves a bit of tranquility during his senior years. This has been in the works for years now, him grooming me to lead. Since I was ten years old, I've known I'd be Capo someday. I'll never forget the elation I felt knowing that one day I'd head up our famiglia's empire. I'll save that for another time. I prefer not to reminisce of my few untainted memories when merely moments before, I strangled a man with my bare hands.

It's liberating, killing a man—especially if he's a fool. It makes witnessing the life drain from their frightened gaze even sweeter. They all underestimate me—my father's enemies—and they shouldn't. I don't have some bullshit nickname like *Bull* or *Cleaner* or whatever the hell else they go by. No, they call me Ruthless. I've earned it and I love seeing them tremble in my wake. I make my father proud and I protect my brothers with my reputation alone.

"Matty, let's go out?" The oldest of my younger brothers suggests it like it's a question. He may want to do something, but he knows to ask rather than demand. They all do. I have six brothers who look up to me and help watch my back; they range in age from sixteen to twenty-nine.

"If we stop, you stay away from anything that isn't alcohol. Understand?"

He grunts, but if he doesn't obey, I'll drag his ass out. I've done it before, and I'd do it again. He enjoys substances too much and I won't let him sink down that path. I won't let him kill himself or disgrace the famiglia.

An hour later and we're at a club, line stretching around the front of the building. We were here the last time we visited Milan; it was packed then too. I rarely take care of business myself outside of New York, but this was a friend of my father's, so it deserved a special trip. Plus, my brother wanted to shop, and it was fashion week. It may sound strange, but when you're a prominent famiglia and frequently in the public eye, what you wear is important. It helps convey the first impression on people and ours radiates power and wealth.

The Vendettis run New York and it's vital that everyone knows it and respects it.

The bouncer nods, waving us through. I roll four deep—myself, my brother, Salvatore, and two of my men. Anyone connected to the life of crime knows who my family is, who I am. I'm important and it's imperative I remain alive until I'm done getting my famiglia prepared for the Capo under me. My own son will eventually take over, but for that to happen, I must have children with someone.

"I need a drink," Salvatore announces, strolling directly for the bar. I let him be. If he's at the bar, he's staying away from the powders and pills that are being passed around like party favors.

With a quick step, I stop a server passing by with a tray full of drinks. She's surprised, a pleased smile gracing her lips, until I down a few of the shots on her tray.

"Hey! Those are for customers. You can't do that."

It's hard to hear over the noise, but after a moment, what she says registers. I've studied many languages over the years, all in preparation.

My father has always said that it's better to know too many languages than not enough. You can't get swindled if you know what they're saying.

Reaching into my front pocket, I hand over two, hundred-dollar bills and take the tray from her grip. I pass it behind me so my men can each have a shot and then I can finish the others off when I'm ready. "Keep it."

She's not fluent in English, but her mouth pops open when she realizes that I just gave her a huge tip. She nods, flashing a timid smile and races back to the bar—I'm assuming to refill her tray before I have a chance to change my mind.

"Thirsty?" I gesture toward the tray of shots, nodding to Vito and Severo. They've earned a drink. They're always cleaning up bodies that I leave behind and making sure no one stabs me in the back—literally.

"Grazie." Severo nods and takes a glass.

"Si." Vito grabs one as well.

I watch as they swallow them back and drink down two more myself. I pass my empty shot glasses to Severo and head for the dance floor. I caught sight of something pretty, something free.

She has deep purple hair and legs that go on for miles. They're right on display, barely covered in a tiny charcoal skirt. It's paired with an obnoxious silver sequin jacket that shimmers as she waves her hands in the air. This new age pop crap isn't dancing; it's jumping around and jiggling your ass.

There's an abundance of multicolor lights shining from above, running over the crowd, painting everyone in a different color. She still stands out with her pink, glittery lipstick and it makes my cock ache just from looking at her. She's dressed for fucking—built for fucking by a man such as myself.

A new song comes on, singing about guys her age not knowing how to treat her or touch her. The woman moves her hips in a rhythm, seducing me with each tilt until I blink and I'm standing in front of her, towering over her. Her winged eyeliner giving her just an edge of mystery behind those big, innocent eyes that practically beg for my attention.

A naughty grin lights her face as she runs a hand down the front of my suit jacket and I pull her in closer. Our bodies brush against each other with each tilt of her hips. It's like she's spinning a spell, paired with the burn from the liquor and my mouth is on hers. Her tongue is made of velvet and sin. The woman can kiss like she was bred for it.

Guys her age don't know how to touch her for sure. I'd never let her out of bed.

The room's hot and stuffy, all the bodies crammed in together on the dance floor, our cocoon even more intimate as her tongue twirls with mine, promising me things she could never keep. Her hands bring mine to her hips and I bend, running them up and over the outside of her thighs.

They're firm and muscular; I know she could ride me if I let her. Or wrap her legs around my waist as I drove into her. She'd be fun. My hands find their way under the hem of her skirt, rubbing, caressing until my fingertips come in contact with her lace-covered pussy lips.

Shoving the scrap of fabric to the side, I thrust two of my fingers inside. Her kiss gets deeper, her mouth telling on her, confessing just how turned on she really is. She vibrates, damn near purring in my mouth as I pump my digits in and out. She's so damn tight; I'd almost swear she was a virgin if she weren't in a place like this, dressed like that.

It takes mere seconds before her mouth is open, moaning loudly, but the music pumps through the building, her beautiful pleasure fading into the night with her orgasm. Her pussy grips my fingers, pulling and throbbing around them, wetness coating my fingers as she comes all over my hand.

Some may call a woman like her a whore, but not me. I'm a dog for pushing her, touching her and making her give in, but I don't care. There's something so unbelievably freeing about a random hookup or a one-night stand in a completely different country with someone you'll never see again. I want to discover every inch of her, leave a lasting imprint she can look back on in five years and still feel me *there*.

"Violet!" is yelled to our side and her lips leave mine, her eyes dazed as she stares at me. My fingers slip free, my lips wet from her kiss. I was just fucking her with my mouth and it was beyond incredible. I probably could've come myself had she not pulled away. Her cheeks are flushed, her lips parted as she pants.

"Violet, we have to go, now!" her friend shouts again, tugging at her elbow. Another girl behind her, gestures in agreement.

"Mr. Vendetti," Vito rumbles and taps my shoulder, calling for my attention. "Your father wishes to speak to you." I nod and turn back toward the woman, but she's no longer there. She and her friends have disappeared just like that, and instead of me leaving an impression on her, she's left one on me.

With an exhale, I toss her image to the back of my mind. It's no use having my men fetch her. As the future Capo, I'm already betrothed. Too bad it's to the Bottaro Princess—a Sicilian—and one of my famiglia's long-standing enemies.

About the Author

Sapphire Knight is a Wall Street Journal, USA Today, and International Bestselling Author of Secrets, Exposed, Relinquish, Corrupted, Forsaken Control, Unwanted Sacrifices, Friction, Unexpected Forfeit, Russian Roulette, Princess, Freight Train(1st Time Love), Gangster, Undercover Intentions, Daydream, Princess, Chevelle, 3 Times the Heat, Baby, The Vendetti Empire, The Vendetti Queen, Cherry, Little White Lies, Ugly Dark Truth, Harvard Academy Elite, 2 Times the Bliss, Heathen, Bash, Opposites Attract, The Vendetti Seven, The Vendetti Coward, Mad Max, Sterling, and Beauty.

The series are called Russkaya Mafiya, Oath Keepers MC, Ground and Pound, Dirty Down South, Harvard Academy, Kings of Carnage MC VP & Prospect, and Royal Bastards MC Texas.

Sapphire's a Texas girl who's crazy about football. She's always had a passion for writing. She originally studied psychology and feels that it's added to her drive in writing. Her books all reflect on what she loves to read herself. When she's not busy in her writing cave, she's playing with her three Doberman Pinschers. She loves to donate to help animals and watch a good action movie. www.authorsapphireknight.com and also find her on Bookbub!

Read more at Sapphire Knight's site.

words to make your *heart flutter*